A FANTASÍA
FOR
TWO LUTES

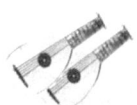

A CHRISTMAS TALE
BY DOUGLAS EVANDER OSWELL

ISBN 978-0-692-93591-0

Typeset by the author in 14-point Adobe Garamond Pro.

Cover art: Bartolomeo Montagna, MADONNA AND CHILD ENTHRONED WITH SAINTS, 1498.

A Fantasia
for
Two Lutes

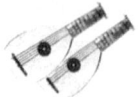
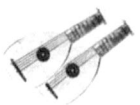

I.

"NO ONE IS DEAD . . . nobody has been killed. I didn't murder her. I didn't kill her after all." Clearly and distinctly these words were uttered by a man named Aaron Westwode, as he lay alone in bed and pondered the reality of a gray December morn, to which the darkness of a still and misty night had given way. Reality felt good, and more than ever now, when it interposed between his waking senses and his dreams. For this bad dream had been a lucid one, and terrifying in its proximity both to the world that he had left upon falling asleep and the one to which his consciousness had presently returned.

So close was it, in fact, that he had tried to reassure himself by constant repetition of those words that first had sprung to mind, upon his realizing — still within the dream, yet on the cusp of waking thought — that it *was* a dream, the same dream that had played inside his brain at random times across the span of fifteen years. A nasty little nightmare, when it came to that, though one whose details he remembered only vaguely. Rain. A furrowed field. A narrow, wooded copse. Thick mud underfoot, conjoined strangely to a sodden, earthen smell. And — horror of it all — the ghastly remnants of an unknown woman he had slain and buried many years before.

Only he *hadn't* killed her, and he *hadn't* buried her, and, in point of indisputable fact, she had never walked the earth. But for the duration of the dream it had appeared to him as if the matter had been settled long before — that indeed he was a killer; that now the truth would out, and he would be exposed at last as the perpetrator of a vile, inhuman crime.

Hard-pressed you would have been to find a less-likely actor for the role. Aaron Westwode a killer? Unthinkable! Aaron was as like to be a killer as the tender infant, sleeping in its mother's arms. No man held a greater reverence for life than he, nor a larger love for all the living things that occupied his world, including even (imagine, if you can!) the human souls who dwelt in it along with him. The very mice, who sometimes found their way into his tiny house and flustered him no end by scurrying about in search of crumbs and leavings they would never find (for his housekeeping was immaculate) suffered nothing worse than being trapped alive and gently manumitted in their proper habitat.

Nor did he look the part. A man of soft, appealing looks was Aaron Westwode, with his handsome, boyish features, large blue eyes, and dark brown hair that sat upon his noble head in a rebellious mass of wavy curls. A man of middle age, with all the strength and health of youth. Not a slight, nor unimposing man, though his movements and demeanor offered nothing to the casual observer suggestive of anything other than the most beneficent forms of kindness, deference and gentility.

Craving solitude, he lived alone, in such a tiny dwelling that a playhouse might have seemed palatial by compare. Imagine if you can a storage shed, sixteen feet by twenty feet in size, and standing tall, not squat, the product of a high and steep-pitched roof that rose above its living space. Imagine if you can the selfsame structure with a red-tiled roof, trim and shutters of a matching hue, and clapboard siding, all of the best construction and repair. Imagine if you can it standing in a graveyard, amidst the wildest scattering of ancient hardwood trees, whose thickened trunks and craggy limbs obscured the sun and lent the house a view it would more naturally have worn if it had stood within the densest wood, and not inside the limits of a small-sized city near an old, historic church. The shack had stood there many years — long before the advent of indoor plumbing and electric power — and once had served to house the sexton of the church and grounds. For generations it had stood unused, much noted as a curiosity belonging to the cemetery proper, with its jumbled-up array of old stone monuments and tombs. For Aaron, unattached, and caring nothing for the approbation or the creature comforts of the world, it seemed an ideal place to live. With that in mind, he arranged with his employer for the right to occupy the place, rent-free, as payment in kind for the capital and labor to be spent on its repair. What once had been an eyesore, soon became a charming, historic and picturesque addition to the church's property.

In perfect balance with the outward aspect that it wore, the inner part of Aaron's house displayed that comfortable vision of cleanliness and order that were the hallmarks of its owner's personality — neither compulsive, nor obsessive, but desirous of peace, stability, and tranquility of the mind. A place for everything, and each thing in its right and proper place. Yet it wasn't that he fussed or fretted over things, but that he naturally, unconsciously assayed to set things right that were amiss. No concerns had he for time. Experience had taught him well that time was of no consequence, or value, in the keeping of a simple man with neither wife nor children — a man who took no interest in the mundane cares and vanities that marked the broader world. He didn't fight it, and he didn't fret about the way it passed.

Except, of course, when time was someone else's, not his own. As sole caretaker of the Old Grace Church (having served in that capacity for fifteen years), Aaron took his duties soberly. His time was fluid, as a laborer whose service stood "on-call" at any hour of the day or night. Thus now (the terror of his nightmare having passed) he set the sheets aside, and sat himself upright with feet upon the floor, eyes closed. He fixed himself in that position five full minutes, then stood up (or rather, hunched up, lest he strike his head against the rafters), made his bed, and descended on a ladder from his bedroom loft above, down to the living space below.

Outside, the dark, gray gloom, and cold, dull atmosphere foretold the coming of a winter storm. Had Aaron owned a television, or a radio, he might have known that light snowfall was on the way. But he owned neither of those things, which he spurned as loud and troublesome intruders on his quiet way of life. In concession to necessity he kept a telephone. But he seldom used it and, because of that, it seldom rang.

The day itself was Christmas Eve, and Aaron had a grave to dig, or rather, finish digging, just outside the churchyard proper on the near end of the cemetery grounds. He had gone to bed in moist weather, tolerably tepid for the time of year, and wakened to more seasonable cold. He therefore lit his only source of heat, a kerosene stove, which adequately warmed the cottage as he took a plain but ample meal of oatmeal, bread and milk. That done, and having washed, he dressed himself in working garb and went outside into the heavy air.

Pausing at the threshold of his house, Aaron cast a long and thoughtful look upon the scenery before him. The church, the churchyard and the cemetery grounds were all historically old. The whole was girded by a solid wall of stone, parts of which had been constructed at the same time as the church itself, although the bulk of it was of more recent provenance. The wall did not extend, however, to the western aspect of the grounds, which ended in a stony, rather steep embankment, beneath which ran a long and lazy river, snakelike in its twisted convolutions, as it slithered on toward the sea. High hills, dressed with woods, rose from the far side of the river, and stood like sentinels, that watched the churchyard and adjacent grounds along their western and their southern ends. Monuments of every size and sort sprang from the earth, like marble mushrooms, nurtured on a ground made fertile by those useless wrecks of human flesh that lay within the earth below, returning slowly to their place of origin. Less metaphorically, perhaps, the oaks and firs that stood amongst the stones had likewise reached their stature through the selfsame agencies of death, corruption, and renewal. Yet their food had once existed in the knowledge of itself, and they did not.

He found the grave as he had left it on the day before, covered up with plywood, and a simple spade protruding from a mound of gray-brown earth nearby. He wasted little time, but pulled the covering aside, took the spade into his hands, and straightaway prepared to dig.

II.

"You had your dream again," observed a rich and honeyed voice, that seemed to have arisen from the chill December air.

Surprised — not startled — at this vocal apparition, Aaron calmly laid his spade aside, turned, and looked to see a comely black man, clad against the weather in a long white coat, and warmly smiling at him with a deferential mien. The coat, and smile, and honeyed voice all belonged to Mr. Indigo, organist of the Old Grace Church, and, as indicated by the smooth and dainty tones with which he spoke, a native of some strange land other than the country where he presently abode. Though his countenance was black as coal, his features were Caucasian: his lips were thin; his nose both sharp and straight. Green were his eyes, and they sparkled with a keen and penetrating light.

"You dreamt your dream again," he said anew, this time looking Aaron straight into his eyes, and giving him a sober gaze, in which the brilliant smile did not depart his face. "It troubled you."

"Good morning, Mr. Indigo," spoke Aaron, in a voice so natural as to suggest that he was not at all bewildered by the insight of the person who had stopped him at his work. "Yes, it came again."

"And did it trouble you?" the black man asked, with yet another sparkle in his green and glowing eyes.

"It troubled me, yes; as it always does."

"Aha, but why?" he cunningly inquired, with a laugh.

"I don't really know," was the reply.

"Oh, don't give me *that*!" exclaimed the black man in a merry tone of voice, as if the whole thing were a private joke between the two. "You're quite an intelligent man, Aaron Westwode, for one whose job is that in which you're presently engaged! Too intelligent for it, a man might say!"

"I don't object to digging graves," rejoined Aaron. "Nor do I object to pulling weeds, or painting posts. It's honest work, it suits my nature, and it gives me all the income that my needs require."

"Which are somewhat frugal, for a man of your attainments."

"My attainments? What attainments, Mr. Indigo?"

"As if you didn't know!" the black man chid, though

not without his imperturbable and smiling air. "I know you, Aaron Westwode . . . know you better than perhaps I know myself. I know what your *attainments* are, and frankly, I believe I envy you — that is, I envy your attainments."

"I want a simple life," said Aaron wearily. "As for those attainments . . ." He shrugged his shoulders. "What are they, really, in the context of the world and what it is? Can they bring clean water to a poor village in a poverty-stricken land, or feed a starving child?"

He leaned upon the handle of his spade, as if he were a cripple and the implement his crutch.

"They are of greater import than you think," said Mr. Indigo. "Of course I *would* say that, given that my own are of a nature much like yours. Music is music, I would make so bold to say, whether it arises from the action of forced air within a hollow pipe, or the touch of human flesh upon a string of gut. And man does not live, or so the saying goes, by bread alone. But yet it puzzles me," he carried on, with a bemused and contemplative air, "why a man of your attainments, given your choice of a low or an exalted way of life, would come to prefer the one above the other. What is digging graves? Has it ever brought clean water to a poor village in a poverty-stricken land, or fed a starving child?"

"No, Mr. Indigo," said Aaron, resignedly. "I'll grant you that it hasn't. Not on any meaningful scale, at any rate. And yet . . . when it comes to that . . . I think . . . ." He faltered now, unable to give voice to his thoughts.

"What you mean to say," said Mr. Indigo, "is that it sets you apart and distinguishes you from the evil forces that appear to rule the world. It puts you on a pedestal of sorts — a *moral* pedestal if you want to call it that — so that you stand above the harsh realities of life, and pompously declare to yourself that even if you *are* powerless to feed the starving child, at least you empathize with him, and assuage your feelings with the soothing thought that *you* were not the cause of his condition. Eh?"

"Yes, Mr. Indigo," he confessed, "Once again, I'll grant that you are right. That's human nature, isn't it? But it's not as if I haven't worked within my sphere to do whatever good I'm capable of doing. Admittedly, it isn't much." He grasped the handle of his spade, as if he would resume his work.

"You give to charity," the black man said.

"As I can," was the reply.

"More than half your income, which, though small, is not, perhaps, so small as one might think. And how much gets . . . *remitted* . . . to your brother, Wolf?"

Despite the tenor of their conversation, neither man

seemed brusque, or short, or out of temper with the other. Though his words were couched in culpatory terms, the black man spoke with smiling equanimity, while Aaron's words and countenance bespoke no outward signs of perturbation or impatience.

"Wolf has certain . . . needs." He spoke the word abashedly, but only slightly so.

"You were such idealists," sighed Mr. Indigo.

"Yes," returned Aaron, "and perhaps still are."

"The world is just the same as when you started out so many years ago. You were his steadfast friend, committed body, mind and soul to him and his beliefs. His beliefs changed nothing. Nor did his great ideals, your fond devotion to him, or even, if it comes to that . . . your actions."

His dark eyes sparkled as he slyly raised his brow.

"What do you know of actions?" Aaron asked him, in a hushed, expectant whisper. At which the black man drew up close to him, and whispered in his ear.

"Everything!"

"*Everything*, Mr. Indigo?"

"Everything. Every thought. Every word. Every deed. From the day that you were born until this very morning, when you had your dream again. Your *special* dream."

"Tell me . . . are you the Devil?" Aaron asked, in so calm a manner that he might have been inquiring whether

Mr. Indigo were the solitary organist of the Old Grace Church.

"The Devil?" cried the black man, with a hearty chuckle, and a big, good-natured smile. "Ha ha! The Devil! That's rich! *So* good!" He laughed out loud, then suddenly, with mercurial velocity, the laughter ceased, and he stroked his chin in studied thoughtfulness.

"On the other hand," he said, "why not? The modern mind perceives the Devil as the antithesis of what's good; a purveyor of evil, and a coveter of souls. Yet, mark this well: *Diabolos* is his name in Greek, or *Satan* as we know him in this day and age."

"The Slanderer," mused Aaron, who had studied Greek. "The Accuser."

"Ah yes! The Accuser! Remember this?"

> *"When winds of conscience waft about thy head,*
> *And brooks of rue do babble in thy brain,*
> *Seek not thy quietude in lonely bed,*
> *Nor utter careful words to stay thy pain.*
> *For though words chosen well may ease the smart,*
> *And turn the wretched, hateful wrong to right,*
> *Alas, in sooth, they cannot touch the heart,*
> *Nor kill Remorse, which rides upon the night,*
> *With Satan, the Accuser, who will steal,*

Betimes to whisper softly in thine ears,
Of dark deeds done: of rack, of cord, of wheel,
And play upon the pipes of hidden fears."

"I wrote those lines," mused Aaron, dreamily, "more than twenty years ago." And with that he finished what the black man had begun:

"Thus torn asunder, none shall see thy strife;
Thy spotted hand; thy bloody, dripping knife."

"Excellent!" chimed Mr. Indigo. "Excellent! Tell me, will I see you this evening at the Old Grace Church?"

"Tonight?" asked Aaron, emerging from a reverie in which he seemed oblivious to speech. "At the church?"

"At half past five," was the reply. "It's Christmas fare, of course. The Reverend Honeybutter doesn't preach on Christmas Eve — he celebrates! You'll hear your friend's ensemble, with an interesting repertoire: late medieval through the Renaissance. Recorders, strings and vocal; that sort of thing. Music for the season. Not bad for a provincial troupe, and amateurs at that. Commit yourself, now. Will you come?"

"Perhaps," was the reply. But it was given noncommittally.

"Oh do!" encouraged Mr. Indigo. "I think you'll find it to your liking. And you might," he said, with sly insinuation, "find it to your liking in a different way than you suppose."

"Do you mean," said Aaron, as he gave a weary sigh, "Melissa will be there?"

"Isn't she always?" was the arch reply. "Besides, why wouldn't she? It's her own ensemble. She has a knack for all things musical. You know, I think she likes you, Aaron."

"I wish for her sake that she didn't."

"You dislike her?"

"I don't dislike her . . . not at all. Miss Honeybutter is a fine example of a woman. She's certainly been good to me. I can't deny it, Mr. Indigo. If it hadn't been for her . . . ."

"Well, let that be as it may," said Mr. Indigo. "But do come, just the same. Don't say no! I can promise you'll be pleasantly surprised, and not just with the repertoire." And he winked, in a devilishly knowing and impishly deliberate way.

As he did, he turned, in the direction of the church-yard. There, no more than forty yards away, could be descried the figure of a woman, clad against the weather in a hooded cloak of black. A surfeit of gold-colored hair protruded from the hood, though of her features, nothing

18

could be seen. She stood before a grave, her eyes cast down toward the ground, as if in thought, or maybe prayer.

"Intriguing, isn't it?" said Mr. Indigo, and it was clear he was referring to the woman with the golden hair.

"Not especially," declared Aaron.

"I believe it is," said Mr. Indigo.

"I don't know why," said Aaron, defensively.

"Because she is so beautiful."

"Not simply beautiful," said Aaron, "but . . . but . . . something that I can't explain, and has to do with light. And every year, on Christmas Eve, she comes to pay a visit to those graves, of a couple by the name of Board, who share a single headstone and who both died on the same day, Christmas Day, now fifteen years ago."

"In a word," the black man said, "intriguing."

"You play upon my mind as you would play upon the organ in the church."

"I am both supremely talented, and supremely endowed by my Creator."

"And who is your Creator, Mr. Indigo?"

"Is there more than one?" He asked the question with a turn of irony, that warped his silken voice.

"Only one true Creator," answered Aaron, with an air of confidence. "Though beneath Him lie a legion of sub-creators, who fashion their own poor works from the perfect reality whose being He has brought to pass."

"Ah!" cried Mr. Indigo, "A philosopher!"

"Not a philosopher, Mr. Indigo, but rather, a student of the obvious."

"Well, we won't go into that," was the reply. "I think you have other things on your mind right now, and I'll not distract you from them." He turned and walked away, down the footpath leading from the cemetery to the churchyard. Abruptly, though, he stopped and turned about.

"Do yourself a favor," he enjoined. "Come to the church tonight. Do not fail to come. It will change your life, I guarantee."

"Very well, Mr. Indigo," said Aaron, resignedly. "Since you desire it so much . . . I'll try."

"Only try?"

"I promise you I'll try."

"Excellent!" And with that word the black man turned again and took his leave. Aaron watched as he retreated down the path, walking jauntily with long and even strides. Just once did Aaron look away, and when he looked again toward the path, Mr. Indigo was nowhere to be seen.

III.

SNOW BEGAN TO fall again, in tiny flakes at scattered intervals. Having placed the plywood back upon the grave, and covering the mound of earth beside it with a canvas tarp, he made his way toward the churchyard and its narrower confines. But as he walked, his eyes inevitably fell upon the enigmatic lady, as into her proximity he came, and neared the place where now she stood in silent reverie.

Loath to interrupt that reverie, he left the path and strayed, as if on purpose, from his goal, walking randomly amongst the scattered graves, and pondering the inscriptions on the stones. Only once did he allow his gaze to fall back to the place where she had been, and when he did he found that she had moved, and now was standing face-to-face with him.

Fifteen times in fifteen years had Aaron seen her there, yet for the first time ever in those years he clearly saw the woman's features, as she paused to let him pass. No bloom of youth did he descry upon that face, yet that she was uniquely beautiful, even in her middle-age, could not have been denied. Not a made-up beauty, but a soft, appealing kind of female loveliness, a grace and elegance composed of quiet virtue, kindly empathy, and physical attraction made manifest by glowing health, a pair of blue and sparkling eyes, and an inner quality of light that glowed forth from the essence of her being.

It was the impression of an instant. Their eyes met, she smiled, and both paused for what seemed a singularly drawn-out period of time.

Suddenly he blurted out:

"Whose are the graves?"

"My mother and my father," she replied, in a voice strangely distant, soft, and kind. Her eyes descended, as her countenance grew dark, but in an instant they were raised, and the luminescent smile returned, as if it were the sun, emerging from a passing cloud.

"And how," inquired Aaron, "did they come to die so young?"

"They died of plague," she said.

"The Christmas plague?" he asked.

"Yes, the Christmas plague," was her reply. "Two of seventeen who lost their lives that year."

"Strange," mused Aaron, "so strange. Thank you for telling me that. Please . . . I'm sorry for your loss. And please forgive my prying. I've seen you coming here for many years, and I've been curious. Too curious, perhaps."

"It wasn't an intrusion," she replied. "My name is Margaret."

"Margaret *Board*?" he chimed.

"Yes," she declared, with a smile.

"My name is Aaron Westwode," he replied. "But pardon my assuming that your parents' name would still be yours. I ought to have supposed it would have long since changed." He reddened as the words came forth.

She smiled and made obeisance, in the manner of a curtsey, not in its exaggerated sense, but with a lovely show of dignity and charm. He returned the gesture with a modest bow.

"Do you work here?" she inquired.

"I'm the sexton of the church," he said. "I keep the grounds, and dig the graves."

"Have you been here long?" she asked.

"Fifteen years," was his reply.

"Fifteen years!" she echoed. "Fifteen years! And have you seen my parents' spirits, wandering about?"

Sadly Aaron shook his head, and cast his eyes toward the ground.

"Nor have I," she mused, at which her features clouded once again. Yet suddenly they brightened, as she looked into his eyes with great intensity.

"If you see them ever," said the woman, with a pleading in her voice, "please, won't you let me know? Please will you be so kind?"

"Yes, of course I will," said Aaron.

"Thank you!" she exclaimed, as quickly she began to draw away. The bright and luminescent smile adorned her face anew. "I have to go now. Thank you, Mr. Westwode. I hope this Christmas brings you peace and happiness."

"And you as well!" called Aaron after her, for already she had moved away. "Wait, Miss Board! Where shall I find you?"

She stopped and turned to face him.

"At the Old Grace Church!" she cried. And then she turned away once more.

She turned away, and Aaron watched as she receded out of sight. She seemed to vanish in and out of view, until at last she could be seen no more. Perhaps that was his fancy, or, less fanciful to one of a pragmatic mind, a product of the snowfall, which now came down in massive, clumping flakes.

Back to the cottage he returned. At its threshold he beheld a wicker basket, bundled up in sheets of cellophane, both red and green. The hamper had been placed there in his absence — a Christmas present from the minister, the Reverend Basil Honeybutter, and his wife. A token of affection, with which they had regaled their sexton each and every Christmas since that year when they had hired him to dig the graves and keep the grounds.

A pleasant little gift, indeed, though one completely

wasted on the object of its giving. The ham and summer sausage were of little use to Aaron, for he ate no meat. The chocolates, the cakes, the nuts and candies likewise were eschewed, as were the tangerines, the oranges and all the other dainties which Mrs. Honeybutter had so thoughtfully, and with such maternal attention to his comfort, packed inside the bursting hamper. And it was not that he disliked those things, so rich, and good, and pleasing to the sense, but that he stubbornly refused to grant himself the right to their enjoyment. The pleasures of the world were not for him. To this he was resolved.

One exception only did he make. An instrument of music lay upon a shelf, beneath the bookcase where his library was kept. No ordinary instrument was this, familiar by name, if not by usage, to the vulgar eye and ear. By name it was a LUTE — a Renaissance lute — whose prototype had flourished in that age of dawning light. Nor was this lute a coarse or mean example of its maker's art. Yet its substance was simplicity itself. Eleven ribs of choice wood comprised a body not unlike a bowl, or half a pear. To it had been fixed a neck, or fingerboard, divided into frets by lengths of gut tied off at intervals, each diminishing in thickness from the one before. Its top, or soundboard, had been fashioned from a sheet of spruce, planed thin and light, and finished with a delicate rosette, carved with exquisite care into a pattern lovely to behold. A tapered box, stuck full of tuning pegs was set upon the neck, and formed an angle to the fingerboard. Such was its construction. A frail and almost weightless thing, adorned with fifteen strings of nylon, gut and wire, grouped in sets, or courses, two in each, except the first which stood alone. A thing of little note, if one looked simply at its parts. Yet, to the eye, its beauty rested in the harmony achieved between those parts, a harmony created by the deft and almost Godlike skill belonging to a master luthier. An impudent imposter of the Deity, he molded his creation from a scattering of elements, that came together through his will to fashion form and beauty from the chaos of the world.

Who was this demiurge? Aaron Westwode could not say. On lutes and their creators he had pondered naught, until that day, twelve years ago, when he had looked to find the instrument outside his door, reposing in a plywood case, exactly like a foundling child abandoned to a stranger's care. This was mystery, not less intriguing for the fact — as Aaron found upon inquiring — that an instrument of this kind and quality might easily have sold for several thousand dollars. Nor did he discover the identity of the person — he must have been a very strange person indeed — who had abandoned it. Nagged by curiosity to guess, the Reverend Honeybutter had come directly, and naturally, to mind. But this the minister denied — denied it emphatically, in fact — and since he was an honest man, his word was given all the credibility that an honest man's word was due. Nor would his daughter own to it, and her word, like her father's, was to Aaron's mind outside the bounds of question. The circumstances of the lute remained beyond his ken, and Aaron let that be as it would be.

Having taken in the orphaned lute, he now resolved to be its foster parent, to the best of his ability. His ability was not to be denied. For Aaron was an educated man, whose schooling had been musical in part, with classical guitar his instrument of choice. The similarities between guitar and lute proved greater than their differences. Goaded on by curiosity, he delved into the wonders of the lute, absorbed its mysteries, and made acquaintance with the music of its time. In this he was assisted by the daughter of the minister, a woman named Melissa, herself a musicologist, with interest in the music of the fifteenth and the sixteenth centuries. She brought him books, and periodicals, and printed music from a varied repertoire. With astounding progress he advanced his knowledge of the lute: its stringing, and tuning, and the historical technique by which it had been played. Soon it was his passion, and the only pleasure he allowed himself.

Now, having washed and changed his clothes, he took

his place upon an antique wooden bench, set the lute upon his lap, cradled it securely in his arms, and plied its fifteen strings. A Fantasy, or *Fantasía,* was the style of piece he played, a free-form work of marvelous invention and remarkable contrivances, delightful to the ear. With artfulness and ease he coaxed sweet music from the instrument, its brittle tones resounding in a thrilling chorus of enchanting voices. With slow and stately tempo he began, in notes that melded unobserved into a lively theme that turned about, measure to measure, in changes both of speed and harmony, until at last he drove the piece to its conclusion in a wild, unfettered show of virtuoso work upon the fingerboard.

But as he played, another human figure, not unnoticed, stepped into his home. Finishing the piece, he set the lute aside, rose up, and looked askance to see a sweet-looking, soft-eyed, buxom young woman, who had opened the door and quietly let herself inside.

"Oh, don't stop!" she cried. "I love to hear you play."

He smiled benignly at his uninvited guest, but made no motion to comply with her request. "Hello, Melissa," he replied, and smiled upon her once again. As well he might, or anybody might, since the sight of the minister's daughter was a pleasant one to see.

She was a pretty woman, with a well-formed figure, high

cheekbones, a rosy-hued complexion and a mass of raven hair; thirty-five years old, and hardly looking twenty-nine. Of ample form, not plump or overweight, she went about with smiling confidence, not born of arrogance, or pride, but of some different cause, far nicer in its inward qualities. Returning Aaron's smile, she took the seat that he had left upon her coming in, and gently — timidly, perhaps — picked up the lute that he had set aside.

"I wanted to wish you a Merry Christmas," she said, with a hint of happy cheer not out of keeping with the sentiment. "And let you know, though you probably don't care, that you're welcome to come to the musical service tonight, our open house afterward, and dinner tomorrow." Her countenance grew darker as she said this, and Aaron looked away, shaking his head as he turned his eyes from her.

"Why won't you ever come?" she asked, appealing. "You're so mysterious, Aaron Westwode; no one can understand you! Why do you stay cooped up in this place, all by yourself, going nowhere and never allowing yourself the simplest of pleasures?"

"If I agree to answer that question," he replied, "will you first answer *me* one question regarding something that I find equally mysterious about yourself?"

"Perhaps," she said. "It all depends on what you want

to know . . . that is to say," she faltered, "in all probability, yes."

"In that case," said Aaron, "I'll ask you why a woman of your youth (for you are still young) and your obvious attractiveness, not to mention your intelligence, your personality, and your talents, has never . . . married." He faintly smiled, and at the same time blushed.

She laughed — no doubt to see the alteration in his hue. Hers was a merry, ringing laugh, that echoed in the bungalow, and filled its empty corners with a larger dose of cheer than could have issued forth from all the Christmas trees in Christendom.

"Because," she said, when her peals of laughter had subsided, "I haven't found a man who suits me . . . who suits me, that is, and is willing to have me." And here she looked exceptionally coy.

"What sort of man would that be?"

"How do you mean?" she asked. "The sort who suits me, or the sort who is willing to have me?"

"Suits you," he replied.

"In a word," she said, "transcendent." And her brown eyes sparkled as she said it.

"Only that?" he asked, incredulous.

"Oh, no! I'm a musician, you know, and fickle to a fault. There are many other qualities I could never do without.

Strength of body . . . strength of mind . . . the strength to do what's right . . . the will to not do wrong. And yet they all arise from that one trait. Give a man transcendence, and I'll know he has those attributes and more."

"Do you know of such a man?" asked Aaron.

"I do," was her reply.

"Only one?"

"Only one in *particular*."

This was followed by a very pregnant pause.

"And I assume," said Aaron, with a knowing smile, "that he's intractable."

"Quite intractable," she sighed, as she turned her eye toward the lute that she had never ceased to hold, endeavoring abstractedly to fret and pluck its strings. She gave it up though, in a trice, for the music she produced was clumsily discordant, hardly worthy of the name, with missed and muted notes. She sadly shook her head. "So much for my ability with the lute," she sighed. "But strings have never been my strength . . . plucked or otherwise."

"You're a competent musician with your voice," commiserated Aaron, as from her hands he took the lute. "And your skill with the recorder is something, I believe, just short of what I'd call professional. I'm surprised, though, that you have such trouble with the lute, considering you've been at it for so long."

"Not long," Melissa said. "A long span of little efforts, I suppose. I don't know what it is. Some deficiency in me, I have no doubt. Anyway," she carried on, "I've answered your question, Mr. Westwode. I haven't married because the right man hasn't made himself available, and I refuse to have anything less. I'm happy, though, to find that you think me attractive and accomplished, even as a spinster. I could, however, say the same for you, despite your being forty-something and a hermit. So, now that I've answered you with candor, what do you say? Why, exactly, are you forty-something and a hermit?"

"I . . . I don't know," he stammered, and was loath to meet her eyes. "I don't think that I can really say."

"Why, then you've lied to me," she said, though not in any way that could have added to his obvious distress. "Don't worry, Aaron, it's nothing." She gently touched his hand. "I'll let you off the hook. That is, if you'll be good enough to play another Dowland piece for me."

Not hesitating, but seemingly glad of her indulgence, he complied with her request, and with a good grace in the act. She listened and she watched, enchanted, as he played the piece called *Lachrimae*, or, *Tears*, one of the most popular musical works of its time. She watched and listened, without embarrassment or consciousness of self. And when the last chord sounded, the *denouement* of all the human woe presented in the tune, she sadly shook her head and heaved a sigh.

"That was beautiful," she said.

"I've got to go now," he returned. "I have to go and see my brother. I think he's dying."

"Would you like a ride?"

"I'll take the truck," he said. "Thanks."

"Will we see you tonight?"

"Perhaps." He sounded dubious.

"We'll look for you," she said, with as much an air of finality in her intonation as if he had actually agreed to come. She smiled at him and left. As she opened the door, a small gust of wind blew flakes of snow inside. The ground outside was coated with a thin, wet covering of white.

Not a minute longer did he stay, but donned his coat at once and went outside.

IV.

ANY APPROACH TO his brother's cabin, other than by foot, would have been impossible. Aaron parked the truck (the church's property, not his) just off the narrow mountain road, and stepped into a world of snow and white-clad evergreen. Looking downward from atop the hill, his eyes could not discern the outline of his brother's meager shack, though it stood not more than fifty yards away. No longer did it snow, although the air was laden still with moisture. The temperature wavered at the point of freezing. Aaron found the narrow path, that zigged and zagged its way across a maze of leafless trees and tangled undergrowth. He cautiously descended, spurning both gravity and the mat of slick, wet leaves beneath his feet. A cold shower of snow from an overhanging limb obscured his view; he took a few steps forward, and when his vision cleared he found himself before the shack. It seemed to have appeared from nowhere.

This was the culmination of a life whose promises had shone so brilliantly. A rude little cabin, built of rough-hewn logs, on land acquired with the money that their parents, now deceased, had spent a life of careful saving to acquire. Larger than the dollhouse in which Aaron lived himself, though nowhere near as picturesque, its wet and blackened walls afforded not a glimpse of comfort, warmth or cheer. Two large crows sat perched upon the roof, croaking in their native tongue some piteous lament. Upon seeing him they flew away, with noisy bustle, and a boisterous flapping of their jet-black wings. And as he watched them go, Aaron noticed that from the rusting chimney pipe, no sign of smoke emerged.

With resolution in his gait, he made his way down to the cabin's door and loudly knocked. With patience he awaited a response. He knocked again, while calling out his brother's name. When no reply ensued he placed his hand upon the knob and slowly drew the door toward himself.

An atmosphere of dark, dank gloom obscured his sight. "Wolf?" he queried, in a low and trembling voice, as his eyes adjusted to the want of light. Venturing inside he saw no occupants — at least no *human* occupants. A large brown cat stared down at him from where it perched upon a shelf, observing Aaron with a sullen aura of distrust. Perceiving its advantage, it bounded from the shelf, and made a dash for freedom through the open door.

Upon the place where it had crouched there lay an envelope. Upon the envelope he saw, scribed visibly in letters large and black, his name: AARON WESTWODE.

Within it was a missive, in his brother's hand. With trepidation he began to read.

Without a change in his expression, or his attitude, he read the letter through until he reached its end, folded it into a square and placed it in the pocket of his coat. Having done so, he directly left the shack, securing the door behind him.

And as he stepped away, the two big crows returned to take the places they had occupied before. The frightened cat lurked nervously about. Once again it eyed him with its sullen attitude. It sprang into the woods as he approached.

Ascending to the road, Aaron reached the truck, climbed inside, and prepared to drive away. His actions were arrested by the vision of a solitary man, clad all in white, who sauntered in a measured pace toward him. He set the parking brake and waited for the man's approach. He came up to the truck upon the driver's side and looked into the window. Directly, Aaron rolled it down.

"He's gone isn't he?" the interloper said.

"Yes, Mr. Indigo, he's gone."

"Dead, I presume?" the black man asked, and showed his white teeth in a little, mocking smile.

"Probably," said Aaron, as he sadly shook his head.

"He should have died hereafter. Not very long hereafter, for his illness was advanced. What would you have given him? A month, perhaps?"

"Perhaps a month."

"It's a blessing for you," said Mr. Indigo. "He was thinking of you, Aaron. Thinking of his brother."

"Strange," mused Aaron in reply. "He said I was his brother . . . he acknowledged it . . . but that . . . ."

Aaron faltered.

"Let me guess," the black man said. "He said that he despised you. Such a lovely thought. He looked upon you as a fool; an irremediable fool, for the superstitions that informed your faith, and your silly sentimentality, which kept him alive, incidentally, far longer than he would have lasted on his own. And did he mention Love? Did he sneer at you on that account as well?"

"You *are* the Devil," said Aaron, quietly. "Or some evil force, incarnate, that has come to earth to torture me."

"Have I ever lied to you?"

"No."

"Attempted to deceive you?"

"No, again."

"Uttered any word to you except the honest truth?"

"No. You never have."

"Then why impugn me?"

"I don't know," said Aaron. "I'm sorry, Mr. Indigo. I apologize. I'm confounded by your knowledge of me, and I'm confused by everything that's happened. I don't know what to do now. Should I go to the authorities, and tell them Wolf has disappeared?"

"He charged you not to. Will you go against his will?"

"No," declared Aaron, after he had paused to think. "I won't. What good would it do? If they find him . . . ."

" . . . then they find him," put in Mr. Indigo. "But I suspect they won't!" His green eyes gleamed. "At least not in a living state!"

"You're right, Mr. Indigo, they won't. Whatever his eccentricities, Wolf was an intelligent man . . . the most intelligent and capable man I've ever known. He said they wouldn't find him. And they won't."

"I'll wager you he took a bus, to some city far away. And blew his brains out in a cheap motel. They may find what's left of him. But he won't be identified. They'll donate his body to research. You understand what that means."

"It's horrible to contemplate," said Aaron, as he hung and shook his head. "But undoubtedly you're right. It's what I would have done myself, if it had come to that."

"Come to what?" the black man asked.

"I don't know. Perhaps the termination of a life that started out with so much promise, but ended in sickness, and in misery, and the disappointment of every goal toward which he'd devoted all his talents, his abilities and all his energies."

"And were they worthy goals?"

Aaron offered no response. The question seemed to shock him. At long last he replied, "Not all of them were worthy. But some of them were noble."

"I'll tell you what," said Mr. Indigo. "You've said that I'm the Devil. Come pay me a visit. Let's drive to Hell together, shall we? On the road paved with those noble ends of which you speak."

"I'm leaving, Mr. Indigo," said Aaron, as he put the truck in gear. "Will you come?"

"What! To Hell?" He smiled, then laughed aloud.

"You may go there if it pleases you. I'm going home."

"I'll see you there," said Mr. Indigo, as from the truck he backed away. "Home, that is, not Hell. Tonight. *At the Old Grace Church*!"

Upon saying which, he touched his hat, and gave a little nod, and jauntily proceeded down the mountain road.

V.

"No one is dead . . . nobody has been killed. I didn't murder her. I didn't kill her after all." For the second time that day he heard himself repeat those words, and for the second time he drew back reeling from their precipice.

He was in the loft again, in bed, not knowing how his being there had come to pass. He tried to rise, but failing in the effort foundered back upon the bed. With a mighty effort in so small a task he opened both eyes wide and looked about. Although the humid cold and leaden atmosphere of earlier remained, the light of day was nearly spent, and night was imminent. Wet snow covered half the window pane. His brother's note lay near him, on the nightstand.

"I must get up," he said aloud. Wearily he rose up to

a sitting posture, feet upon the floor. Ten minutes he remained in that position. And when the time had ended,
he exhaled a lengthy sigh and burst into a sob that made
his body shake.

He took the letter up and read. The words flowed in a
dark, and cold, and melancholy stream.

I am off to meet my maker — that is to say, Nobody from the land of Nowhere. Dying is a bore.
While it's theoretically amusing, in the actual event
it's tiring in the extreme. Though pain is stimulat-
ing, one grows weary of its endless, nagging presence. I'm resolved to put an end to the ennui. At
some point, probably before you read this note, I
will have disrupted the simple chain of cause-and-
effect which you call life, and I call a stupid inter-
lude between two long periods of nonexistence.
The instrument is close at hand. A simple motion
of the finger — all is done. Then, nothing. It would
be nice to think that one could finally disprove
that mindless rubbish which you and all your fel-
low fools insist upon, despite all evidence there's
nothing to it — that there was never anything to it
— and that your god is a delusion, nothing more.
I'm happy that it isn't possible. Ecstatically happy.

You are, of course, a perfect fool. I say that in all affection, since it's the only means I have of flattering you. I don't think I would have liked you half so much if you'd had any brains. You certainly wouldn't have been as useful, and you WERE useful, believe me. I'll spare you a recitation of just how useful you were, but you can take pride in the thought that you might have earned yourself a flyspeck of a place in history.

And I suppose I ought to thank you for all your help while I've been sick and dying. But why? You did it out of love, of course, and brotherly affection, which are two of the stupidest reasons for doing anything. And it isn't just the sentiment that irks me, but that you had ulterior motives. You really did it for your nonexistent god, and the groveling devotion you reserve for him alone . . . .

He could read no more, but weakly tossed the note aside. It fluttered to the floor. "I must get up," he said beneath his breath. "I must get up."

Once again he tried to rise, and failed. Again he spoke aloud, softly and monotonously reciting verse that he had written long ago:

A Fantasia for Two Lutes

When winter's snow descends upon the land,
And pall of sullen drab all light beshrouds,
Behold this wretched face; these feeble hands;
These eyes, reflecting gloom of passing clouds.
Had I but faith enow (but I have not),
Vast mountain peaks to cast into the sea,
To touch Death's icy flesh and make it hot,
Forevermore to know my grave were free,
Then would I slay this melancholy blight,
Which binds my soul in ribands cast of blue,
And morning wrest from sempiternal night,
As from the crypt I stumbled, born anew.
But faith will not suffice to raise my head.
Futility! I would that I were dead.

Suddenly, with new-found strength, he rose, and climbed down from the loft. With forceful resolution in his gait he made his way into the kitchen at the far end of the house. From a block of knives he drew one with a long and gleaming blade. Placing its point at the side of his throat, he closed his eyes, held his breath and grimaced, as though determined in that moment to drive it through his flesh. He faltered momentarily, and as his eyelids opened once again, the orbs they shaded fell upon the lute, the lute of mystery, reposing on its shelf.

"I know you now," said Aaron, as he crossed the room. He seized the lute and clutched it rudely by the neck, holding it before his face and lashing out in bitter tones, both angry and accusing. "I know who sent you here . . . HIM ! Damn you!" Aaron cried, as forcefully he dashed the lute against the floor. "Damn you! Damn you! Damn you!"

Then, abruptly, all his rage was spent. An eerie stillness draped itself around him like a shroud. Quietly, incredulously, he knelt before the shattered ruins of the object that had given peace and comfort to his soul.

"I have killed my child," he said.

Holding the broken remnants to his breast, he noiselessly wept. He vented his grief thus several minutes, and then upon an instant he stoically left off, ashamed, perhaps that he had given way, and gathered up the tangled mass of splintered fragments.

In doing so, his eye beheld an object he had failed to see for all the years that he had owned the lute, and might not ever have been seen, even had he troubled himself to peek through the weavings of its beautifully-carved rosette into the depths of its interior. That object was a piece of parchment, glued to the inside of the middle ribs that formed the body of the lute. A modest scrap of vellum, upon which had been scribed three words:

A Fantasia for Two Lutes

CHARLES BOARD, LUTHIER.

Music emanated from the darkness at the far end of the room. It was the music of the lute; not of one lute, but of two, and the piece was Johnson's *Flatt Pavan*. A man and woman sat together, nearly tête-à-tête, upon the antique wooden bench. Each played upon a lute, and each took loving glances at the other as they played. A strange light shone above their heads, a faintly glowing emanation by which Aaron could see the details of their faces and their forms. A handsome couple, not old, but in the final years of middle age: the man of sturdy build with graying temples and a balding crown; the woman tall and stately with high cheekbones, silver hair, and fair complexion, unchanged by her years. Distinct and clear their music echoed through the quiet house, as each lute alternated flawlessly from melody to ground, one lute speaking to the other, and the other making answer in its turn.

Aaron watched in fascination as they wrought the piece to its conclusion, unable to take his eyes from the eerie spectacle before him, or his mind from the slow and haunting melody they played. The piece was not a lengthy one, and when the last chord faded out the pair regaled each other in one final loving glance, at which the woman turned her head aside, looked Aaron in the eyes, and smiled a Mona

Lisa smile. She turned her head away, then, in a heartbeat, both were gone.

No alteration had he made in his position while the spectral performance had been played before his eyes. Nor had he ceased to hold against his breast the ruins of the lute. Yet now he looked to find the instrument restored to life, as whole and sound as it had been before his act of rage. With utter incredulity he ran his hands about its form, alternating the motion with unbelieving glances at the empty bench. No, not completely empty. A small, almost insubstantial object lay there, where he had seen the apparition, hardly visible in the gloom from which the ghostly light had fled.

It was the parchment he had found inside the lute. Bearing the name of its creator.

"I must speak with her," he said aloud. He fondly kissed the lute, placed it carefully inside its case, and then, abruptly, set out for the Old Grace Church.

VI.

DARK NIGHT MASKED the gloom of day, as falling snow renewed its native vigor, drifting earthward, unimpeded by the smallest breath of wind. A flight of geese passed noisily, unseen, overhead. An inch of untouched snow lay underfoot, illuminating with a cold and shining glow the prospect of the graveyard, and all that stood in its proximity.

Music issued from the Old Grace Church, faint and scarcely audible. The nearer Aaron walked towards its source, the louder it became. At last he recognized a Christmas song, *Adeste Fideles*, played upon the small pipe organ that was the pride and joy of the church. The organ played exclusively by Mr. Indigo.

"You couldn't do it, eh?"

The black man stood before him, decked out dandily in white.

"No. I couldn't. Or rather . . . something happened to prevent it."

"It's just as well," said Mr. Indigo. "It would have been a sin to take your life . . . a life that isn't yours to take."

"I didn't do it," Aaron said.

"Ah, no, you didn't," he replied. "Something happened to prevent it. *But you were going to!*"

The organ ceased, and for a few brief moments no sound at all could be perceived. It started up anew, with *Hark, the Herald Angels Sing*, still muted by the thick stone walls of the edifice from whence it came.

"Where are you going with your lute, this snowy night?" the black man asked.

"I am going to the Old Grace Church."

"I knew you would," said Mr. Indigo. "Perhaps I'll see you there."

"Perhaps?" mused Aaron. "But . . . the organ. Who is at the organ now?"

The black man smiled.

"I am there," he said, at which he burst into a laugh. Then he turned and walked away, down the footpath, in the opposite direction of the church.

Not wishing to pursue him, Aaron made his way toward the church, walking along the tree-lined path toward the soft, pale light that shone from four tall windows that adorned the south side of its nave. The church was a cathedral in miniature, with gray stone walls, constructed in the cruciform style and oriented west to east, with its entrance on the same side as the river's bank. It boasted both a belfry, and a miniature transept, lending it the form and aspect of a cross. Not a large establishment, as churches went, but one designed, perhaps, with something more than worldly thoughts in mind.

He stood inside the vestibule alone. The organ's strains still sounded in his ears, much louder now, as they echoed from the rafters of a nave that seemed alive with warmth, and light, and human presence.

His lute-case still in hand, Aaron entered in upon a gathering of people, waiting for the service to begin. The pews were not quite full. Perhaps at one time, in the long and varied history of that church, they had been filled to overflowing — but these were different days. In the sanctuary, resting on a table, he spied a row of instruments, like his lute the modern counterfeits of antique prototypes. Before the altar stood a row of chairs, arranged in a semicircle, with its concavity facing out toward the nave.

On the left-hand side of the sanctuary, nestled away behind the pulpit, yet visible to everybody present, stood a small pipe organ, ringed around with wooden balustrades. A man sat at the organ playing, his profile manifest, and his body moving ostentatiously in concert with the music he was drawing from its windy depths. The piece was *Silent Night*. The instrumentalist was Mr. Indigo.

With no hint of surprise, or hesitation in his gait, Aaron walked softly down the center aisle and took his place within an empty pew. He could see the black man as he played, his form obscured but slightly by the modest pulpit. He watched and listened as the echoes of the music died away, leaving a peaceful silence punctuated only by the sound of quiet coughing and the whispers of the listeners assembled.

Then upon a sudden, the organ pealed anew. Not a Christmas song, nor anything befitting the occasion, but the opening chords of William Byrd's *Fancie in C Major,*

No. 2. It jarred the senses, coming hard and loud upon the heels of quiet Christmas fare. With puzzled looks the people glanced at one another, a questioning bemusement in their eyes.

And so the black man played, with skill both wondrous and bizarre. Like a demon of the stops he plied the keys, and drew out voices beyond the limits of the instrument he played; beyond the bounds of any human touch. The music told a story not in words, but in the language of the human soul. And when at last the piece was done, and the echoes of the final notes had died out in the rafters overhead, the black man closed his music-book and rose, faced the congregation, smiled, and gave a humble bow. Then, the music-book beneath his arm, he briskly stepped into the crossing, turned, and made his exit through the transept door, vanishing without a coat into the snowy night.

At once the lights went dim, and as they did, the droning hum of bagpipes sounded from behind. Every head at once was turned about. A pair of pipers stood inside the vestibule, piping out the old Medieval tune of *Angelus ad Virginem*. When they had played the first part through, new sounds were heard in the opposite direction, and once again the congregation turned. A gathering of performers had quietly come in, and taken their positions up, as if upon a stage.

There in the sanctuary, before the altar, a chorus was assembled, joined by instrumentalists with their pieces at the ready. Seated in the semicircle were the instrumentalists, with the choristers arranged behind.

Near the center of the semicircle, Melissa sat amongst the instrumentalists, holding a recorder, to which she now applied her lips, as the droning of the pipes subsided and the modest chorus sang in Latin verse.

> *Angelus ad virginem,*
> *Subintrans in conclave,*
> *Virginis formidinem,*
> *Demulcens inquit, Ave!*

He saw her then. Beside the pastor's daughter, seated to her right; a lute in her embrace. Margaret Board, the woman in the graveyard. The woman he had come to find, to tell her of the vision he had seen.

She sat there near Melissa, clad in a narrow-waisted dress of black, which reached below her knees and formed a striking contrast with her fair complexion, and the golden hair that hung in loose curls to her shoulders, wild and free, yet not by any means unkempt. An ethereal light, its origin unseen, shone down upon her figure, bathing her, and the instrument she played, in a soft stream of glowing incandescence.

Incredible music was being played. A beautiful performance, artfully conceived, of antique Christmas carols, unfamiliar to the modern ear, yet powerfully appealing both to mind and soul. Exotic instruments, married to the human voice, vied amongst themselves in offering their tribute both to Concord and the Season. Exotic songs, some grave in their devotion to the time, some loud and raucous in the glad anticipation of revelry and feast, proclaimed the birth of Christ as they had sung it in an age where filth, disease and famine showed themselves in hard, unyielding contrast to the beauty, and the wonder, and the mystery of Art.

Second to nobody's was Aaron's admiration for that Art. Yet its pleasures and enchantments now were lost on him. For his mind stood fixed upon the woman with the lute, a lute which looked, for all the world, exactly like the one that he possessed.

With marvelous alacrity she played. The lute was clearly audible as well, as if some unseen power had raised its voice over and above its normal, quiet sound. With no sensation of the passing time he watched her play, transfixed. Then, abruptly, bright light filled his eyes. For a fleeting instant he removed his gaze from where it had remained unchanged, then looked again to see the troupe no more. Margaret had disappeared. The congregation, too, was gone from sight.

"Why don't you seek her at the pastor's house?" the black man said. Aaron turned to see him sitting in the pew, within a church grown noiseless, and void of all presence save the two. "Certainly they'll all be there. Look . . . her lute is left behind."

And so it was. Upon the altar lay the lute, behind the place where Margaret had sat. Mr. Indigo had vanished out of sight, and Aaron stood immersed in pouring snow, before a large and many-gabled house, from which the sounds of merriment came forth.

VII.

"The strangest thing I ever heard!" exclaimed a fat man with a ruddy face, as he delved into a plate of chicken livers wrapped in strips of bacon. "Bubonic plague? But how could they have missed it? The symptoms are distinct."

He stood within a room, or rather, in the entrance to a room, where several men, the minister among them, sat and stood, discoursing in the presence of a glowing fire. Pleasing was the warmth within this room, though not less pleasing than the friendly warmth that seemed to radiate all through the spacious house, alive with light and human presence, not only in the place wherein he stood, but every other room as well.

"Oh, they caught it in the end," said Reverend Honeybutter. "There were several cases after, but they all survived. My understanding is that it's relatively easy to treat if you know what you're dealing with, and don't waste any time. Correct me, Doctor, if I'm wrong."

"That's the trouble with physicians in provincial towns," observed the man of medicine, peering thoughtfully into a glass of wine, as if he were an oracle, a priest of the divining arts. "We play percentages in everything. The paradigm is king. No one can avoid it, and I'll not exclude myself, although I try to keep an open mind. But all too often it happens. If the patient fits the paradigm, then everything is fine. If not, well, he can kiss . . ." (here he paused and glanced up at the minister) ". . . bid himself farewell."

Reverend Honeybutter laughed, and all the others joined in. "I wouldn't place you in that class, Dr. Rauchfife," he said, and a chorus of voices sang out a broad assent.

"The problem was," resumed the sage, his instrument of divination still in hand, "that in this instance all the planets were aligned to produce a calamity from what in ordinary circumstances would have come to nothing. On the twenty-third of December a snowstorm hit the region. It was unlike anything that had been seen within the memory of anybody living at the time. You say you made this wine?"

"I most certainly did," the minister replied. "And the Belgian ale as well."

"Strange occupations for one of your profession," said the man of corpulent dimensions, still addressing the hors d'oeuvres.

"Just following the practice of its Founder," was the minister's reply. "Minus the miracle, of course. Then again, if it's a miracle you want, just look upon that glass of ale, or that dish of chicken livers, or that fire in the grate. Physical reality is a miracle. We're awash in miracles, though we never recognize them as such, because we're born into their midst, and take them all for granted."

"Why, that's our sermon for the day!" the plump man cried. "I was wondering if we'd have it."

"In that case," muttered Dr. Rauchfife, whose story had been cut short, "I'll have another miracle . . . another glass of wine, that is." From a bottle near at hand he helped himself.

"It was a storm," he carried on, "unlike anything that had been seen within the memory of any person living at the time. Coming on the back of a powerful Nor'easter and dumping two feet of snow in driving winds and piercing cold. Everything shut down . . . literally, everything stopped dead in its tracks. No need to dwell on details. But that was the deciding factor. The very afternoon before it hit, a middle-aged woman showed up at her doctor's office with chills, headache, fever and . . . swollen lymph nodes. I won't name her doctor . . . some of us knew him, but he's now deceased. The patient was a technician at a veterinary practice."

"Oh dear!" exclaimed the gentleman of size. "I think I see where this is going."

"Indeed," said the physician, as he cleared his throat. "A man had shown up several days before with a very sick cat that was suffering from septicemia — severe blood poisoning. What they didn't know, or perhaps couldn't have imagined was that the poor little cat had plague. Now plague, in modern times, is not an easy thing to catch. It rides in the digestive tracts of fleas, which ride in turn on the bodies of warm-blooded animals, whose blood they suck. When a flea drinks the blood of a plague-infected animal, the bacteria start to multiply in its gut. It does so until by sheer numbers it stops up the digestive system of the flea, making it ravenously hungry, and at the same time increasingly mobile as it frantically looks for food. And if its host animal should die, as invariably it does . . . ." He paused and looked about.

"Why then, it hops on something else," said Reverend Honeybutter.

"Bingo!" cried the doctor. "Which apparently is what happened. The cat was put to sleep, and its carcass lay about, uncovered, in a back room, waiting for disposal. The practice was a large one, with ten employees, not counting three vets. All four persons who had been in contact with the cat got sick — bitten by infected fleas. A fifth person, who had visited his vet next day, was also taken ill. As was a sixth, who was nowhere near the practice, but had transacted business with one who had. All cases of bubonic plague. None of them reported ill, except the technician who had gone to see her doctor. *She* was diagnosed . . . with cat scratch fever."

"Cat scratch fever!" cried several listeners in chorus.

"Not as preposterous as it seems. At least at the outset the symptoms are the same. Malaise . . . fever . . . swelling of the lymph nodes . . . headache. And of course, the woman worked in a veterinary practice, and had been bitten by a cat the week before. They never could have known that it was plague, especially in these parts . . . it simply doesn't happen. Come to think of it, that diagnosis was probably the best they could have made. Cat scratch sickness is usually benign and clears up by itself. So they sent the patient home without prescribing anything stronger than bed rest, fluids and something for her headache. Come back, they said, if things get worse. And so she would, I have no doubt. She went home. Everyone went home. Then the blizzard came."

He paused and cleared his throat, then took a sip of wine.

"White Christmases are very pleasant things, when the snow is fresh and new, and there's just enough of it to pretty up the scenery. They're something else again when the wind blows down your power lines, and the snow blocks off your roadways, and traps you in your home, cut off from all connection with the outside world. By the time the roads were cleared and power was restored, seventeen people had died of plague, including two entire families. Some of them succumbed when the bubonic form of the disease became pneumonia, which in plague is the most virulent form it takes. One survivor lost both legs to gangrene, another nasty consequence of plague, when it poisons the blood."

"And where did it originate?" the fat man asked.

"No one ever knew," was the reply. "The snow stayed on the ground until late March, and by the time the last of it was gone, all evidence of where the illness came from vanished too. It all seemed to have started with the cat, but where the cat got plague is anybody's guess. Probably from a rat."

"And where did the rat get it?" Reverend Honeybutter asked.

"From a flea," replied the doctor.

"And the flea?"

"From another rat."

"Ah, I see!"

"And I'm not trying to be a tease," continued the physician, as he helped himself again to wine, "but that's the way it's been for ages, in a ceaseless cycle. The crux of the mystery is why it happened here, in this cool, damp climate. And the best answer anyone can give is that it was just a freak of nature; a one-in-a-million chance. Cold comfort to the ones who died."

"Two of them are buried here," observed the minister, "in the cemetery right outside the wall. Mr. and Mrs. Board, instrument makers, who owned a workshop in the hills. Nice people; respectable people. Not members of our church, but fairly well-known in the area. We donated the plots — everyone was knocking himself out to help — sadly, though, they never found . . . hello, dear!" He beamed as he beheld his pretty daughter, who had come into the room, a plate of sandwiches in hand. She was immediately attended to by the fat man, who had been listening with rapt attention to the story of the plague, while consuming chicken livers with astonishing dexterity. He took the platter from her hands, as if he claimed it for his own, set it down, and made obeisance with an ostentatious bow.

"Oh, what glorious music!" he cried, with enthusiasm that appeared sincere. "I could listen to you all night! Beautiful performance . . . beautiful performers!"

"Thank you, Mr. Forrest," she replied, and smiled a bright and most bewitching smile. "And you seem to like those chicken livers just as much!"

"Ah well, the liver *is* the best of it!" opined that man, as he rubbed his hands with hedonistic glee. "Of the chicken, that is. And the best part of the goose as well! You haven't any more now, have you, dear?" He smacked his full, thick lips and seemed to leer at her. She gave a chiding glance and moved away.

Strange to say, she passed by Aaron as he stood within the entranceway, without a word of greeting, or any intimation that she saw him standing there.

And now he moved, or rather, drifted, down a lighted corridor, toward a lofty room, not unlike a ballroom, whence a crowd of persons stood assembled, enjoying themselves in a merry euphony of blithe and mirthful sound. There he saw, amongst the people gathered, the musicians of Melissa's troupe, some of whom had come together 'round a Christmas tree, and played impromptu music on a trio of recorders. He stopped before a table, bountifully laden with glasses of a swarthy-colored wine, a wicker cornucopia bursting with ripened fruit, a platter of meats and cheeses, and in the center of it all, a crystal bowl of steaming punch, ruby-red, and fragrant with the smell of cinnamon.

"Won't you try the sherry? It's an Oloroso; very rare." Mrs. Honeybutter stood beside him, plump and pretty like her daughter, though her hair was gray, and her rounded features tinged (but slightly) with the lineaments of age. She proffered him a tapered *copita*, and from her hand he took it, holding the glass by its stem, as one accustomed to its use. "It's Christmas, Aaron, dear. Drink, and celebrate!"

Timidly he placed his lips upon the glass and sipped. The Oloroso shocked his senses, both of smell and taste: mildly sweet, yet pungent with a thousand rich and subtle tones — a Christmas pudding in a glass, the heat of spirit full upon it. He sipped, then drank, then quaffed. Mrs. Honeybutter beamed upon him, smiling her approval.

"You must have more," he heard her say, as from a hand he took a second glass. But he took it from a different hand than that which had given him the first.

"It's an Oloroso; very rare," the black man said, and followed it with verse, a verse he sang in smooth bass tones:

A Fantasia for Two Lutes

Most men do love the Spanish wine,
For that will make their brains more fine,
Called Sack-O cum Sugar-O!

"A lovely wine, and very dear," he said, in his most condescending voice. "*Trink aus*! And let not your pleasure be disturbed by any thought of what it cost, and how the money might have gone to help the poor! For as you know, the poor are with us always!"

He deeply drank again, and set the glass down drained. "Come!' cried Mr. Indigo, taking him by the arm and leading him away. "Come along with me! I want to show you something!"

The light, and warmth, and gaiety were gone, as now the black man led him to a sector of the house that he had never seen before, of many rooms and quiet corridors, all cold, and dark, and moist with the clammy air. Before one door the black man paused, and held his hand aloft.

"Stay!" he cried. "You *would* go in there, would you? *She* is there, you shameless man! Have you no sense of shame?"

Aaron paused, and quietly withdrew the hand that he had placed upon the knob.

"She is there," the black man softly said. The cold and empty hallway echoed back his words. Aaron placed his hand upon the knob again. He turned the knob and pushed upon the door.

VIII.

WITHIN THE CHURCH he stood alone, in darkness of an otherworldly depth. Within the vestibule he stood, and listened to the soft, enchanting sound that issued from the nave, behind a heavy set of doors, whence reason cried that it could not have come at all, for it was the voice of a solitary lute. Indeed, it *was* a lute, and even though it seemed impossible, he recognized the melody as the opening *diferencia* of *O Gloriosa Domina*, that pæan to the Virgin Mary, whose notes had issued from the fertile mind of Narvaez, a master of the Spanish lute, who lived and flourished in the sixteenth century.

> *O Heaven's glorious mistress,*
> *Enthroned above the starry sky,*
> *Thou feedest with thy sacred breast,*
> *Thine own Creator, God most high.*

Carried through the dense black mantle of the air in which he stood, the ringing notes, with sorrowful and plaintive harmony, beguiled his mind with beauty unalloyed by the sense of sight. He stopped and listened through the first and second *diferencias*, while every other sense that he possessed held still, and naught remained of his perceptions but the faculty attuned to sound, and the glimmer of an understanding past the realm of thought.

And when the last chord of the second *diferencia* rang out, bell-like in its clarity, and echoed in the empty nave, his sense of self returned. The third *diferencia* began. Only slightly did he hesitate. Opening the door, he stepped into the space beyond.

He saw the woman seated in the place where she had sat before, the lute enfolded in her arms. She sat before the altar, underneath the cross, illumined by a spectral light; a light whose glow revealed the forms of objects near at hand, yet past whose borders nothing could be seen. Black and empty was the space outside the margins of her light. Within the void he saw nothing of himself, nor any portion of the path he trod. Pure was the light beyond. Pure was the music that the lady played. The verse that he had known, so long forgotten, stirred within his mind.

What man had lost in hapless Eve,
Thy sacred womb to man restores,
Thou to the wretched here beneath,
Hast opened Heaven's eternal doors.

He sat before her now, his lute reposing in his arms. The music now was his. She followed him with gentle eyes, as all the while her strange, uncanny light continued to shine forth. From the works of Narvaez he played, *La Canción del Emperador*, the song of sorrow for a love bereaved.

> *A thousand regrets for abandoning you,*
> *And leaving behind your loving face.*
> *I feel such sadness and such painful woe,*
> *I think my days will dwindle soon away.*

"I have been sick," he said. "Very sick, for a very long time, though I never knew it until now."

Nothing did she say. But she affirmed it in her eyes.

"I supposed that I was well. I couldn't tell that I was sick. The sickness crept upon me by degrees, in changes that came slowly, all too slowly, day by day. And now today it came to me, as if to one who sees through glasses for the first time in his life, when all the while his vision has been poor."

Still she answered nothing in reply. Pity and compassion could be read upon her face, and she looked upon him as a mother might behold a child in pain, with tenderness and woe.

"I wished to kill myself. The world grew dark in every

way. I felt myself entombed alive within a grave of black despair. I told myself that all the good to which I had aspired was simply an illusion, a product of my self-deceit. I knew that I was bad, as evil and corrupt as everything within my view. I broke my lute. I smashed it into pieces on the floor. The knife was at my throat. I paused. And then I saw . . . the mother and the father whom you told me of. They sat before my eyes and played their lutes." He paused, unable for the time to carry on.

"As they often did," she said, in tones as sweet and gentle as the voice of the lute she played.

"I have been sick," he said again. "But as I look upon you now, I feel as if I might some day be well. I couldn't kill myself. I saw your parents and I thought of you, and that thought led me here. To see you, and to hear you speak. To hear you tell me who and what you are, and why you've led me here, although I came here of my own free will." He looked at her, imploring her, with every aspect of his face.

Silence followed once again. Suddenly she spoke.

"Once I was a creature of this world. No longer is that so. Fifteen years ago that body died of which I was possessed. To speak it in your human words, I am a ghost."

"A ghost!" he echoed, in a voice half-between a whisper and a cry. "But then, you must be . . . dead."

"You contradict yourself," was her reply, "I *am* dead, yes . . . but only in those words to which your mind is held in thrall. 'Am,' is a state of being. That which *is dead*, cannot *be* dead, for by its definition it no longer *is*. Rather say that what I *was* is dead and gone, yet what I *am* is not."

"You astonish me!" he cried.

"Stay with me," she said, "and you will be astonished more than once. You ask me why I've led you here. Come, I'll show you! Take your lute and play!"

He did as he was bade. She played her lute, and Aaron joined her. The piece was bright and fast, a short and pretty lute duet called *Drewries Accordes*, which he had never played before. He could not say how he knew the notes and chords belonging to his part, for he had no tablature to guide his hand. Yet play his part he did, and with the ease of one who knew it well. In perfect sympathy they played. He presently was in a different place, walking solitary on a country road, in dry and tepid weather, on a golden afternoon.

IX.

NOT EVEN THE change from womb to world, that shocking transformation which all must undergo, could rival the wonder of the sudden alteration in every sense he owned. Like a mildly drunken state, in which the senses shrink into the self, freeing thought from their insistent prate, it filled him with a beautiful euphoria which, though new, seemed somehow familiar, as if he had experienced it before, at some unknown point in an unremembered past. Light without heat. Sound without vibration. Touch without discomfort. All of it present, yet none of it relayed through the organs most commonly allied with those phenomena, but by some strange, inscrutable conveyance, directly to his conscious self.

It seemed to him as if it were a mist. Not a mist of obscuration, but of clarity.

He walked in open country, on a winding lane, amidst a rolling landscape carpeted with fields of tall and ripened grain. Soft, yet fulsome, was the light that shone on all sides from some hidden source, for no sun could he see. Yet every object cast a shade, in heavy contrast to the yellow brilliance of that sunless light. Quiet was the air; so very still that not a stray leaf danced, though leaves aplenty strewed the path he trod.

Above him, in the hills beyond, he saw a house, half-hidden in the trees. Some appealing intuition, a novel way of understanding, hitherto unknown, impelled him now to move toward that place.

Then, in the contemplation of the act, he found himself before the house, astounded at the change in time and space that seemed to be a consequence of will, but not of any action fostered by that will. A large house, well-maintained, and clad in cedar shakes, stood silent and alone within a grove of pines, whose fallen needles carpeted the ground beneath his feet. Not far distant stood a second building, smaller than the first, and oblong, with a one-pitch roof. Its door swung to-and-fro. An air of desolation hung about the place. The want of human presence, in a setting made for human presence, seemed to make it so.

The door now swung toward him. He held his hand out to arrest its motion, yet curiously, the hand did not make contact with the door. He stood inside the building now, and looked to see the contents of a well-used workshop, its shelves and benches littered with the curious implements of the woodworker's craft. Three lutes, of varying designs, depended from a rack in a corner of the shop, while the body of a fourth lay half-constructed on a chiseled mould, its ribs arrayed in alternating woods both light and dark. Fresh wood shavings lay scattered all about, while on a second bench reposed the soundboard of another lute, with its intricately-carved rosette — a thing of beauty in itself, though it was but the portion of a whole.

"Father, will you come inside?" A voice sounded close at hand, and with that voice came another change. Two figures occupied the room. A man now sat, an implement

in hand, and worked upon the soundboard with the con-
centration of a master luthier, whose two hands wrought
his mind's intentions flawlessly upon the yielding wood.
A young, fair girl, seventeen perhaps, stood nigh him. He
paused his work, looked up into her eyes, and smiled a
smile of unalloyed pleasure. As well he might, for she was
beautiful.

"Father won't you come inside? It's well past noon."
Aaron heard the young girl's voice, not with ears, but by
some unknown faculty both strange and new, yet highly
pleasing to his sensibilities. Father and daughter did not
perceive his presence, but carried on as if alone.

"In a bit," he said.

"But you've been here all the morning long!" she remon-
strated. "Come and have your lunch at least."

"I will," he gently said. "I know I've been spending all
my time at work. That's the worst part of being in business for yourself and having no one else to help. If the
work came steadily I could do it at my leisure, but it always seems to come in waves, and I can't turn any of it
down. I've got orders for nine lutes, two Renaissance gui-
tars, and one orpharion for Mr. Pilkington. Truly a thing
of beauty, if I don't mind saying so myself! And the timbre
. . . . well!"

The young girl smiled.

"It doesn't yet exist," she said, "and yet you speak of it as if it does."

"Clever of you to point that out," the man rejoined. "I could say it's only a way of speaking, but you know, my dear, it really *does* exist. The reality of the thing is in my mind. Having gotten there, it comes to have a sort of immortality, greater even than its form will be, when once it's built. That said, I doubt that Mr. Pilkington will pay the balance of his order for a thought. Margaret, what day is it?" he asked.

"It's Saturday, of course!" she said.

"Of course? There's no 'of course' about it! To me, one day is just the same as every other. They all seem to meld together into one another and form one big . . . continuum. Do I care? What do *you* think, dear? Do you think I care?"

She laughed. "I think you could never be so happy as when you're here all by yourself, playing God with bits of wood. Therefore," she continued in a merry, scolding way, "don't let me hear you complain about not knowing what day of week it is, or the impositions put upon you by your *paying* customers."

"Well, well; I *won't* complain," he said. "*Can't* complain either, when it comes to that. Maybe you'd like to join me some day? We could make a go of it together; a father-and-daughter enterprise."

"I don't know," the young girl stated, in a noncommittal, though reflective, way. "I know I could be happy doing it. But . . . I think I'm more inclined to *play* a lute than *make* a lute."

"Have you made your mind up, then, at last?"

"I think I have," was her demure reply.

"Well, I'm disappointed," he said. "But only because I'm selfish, and not because I don't think it's a better thing for you to do. Your judgment was always good, even as a child. And to deny the world a talent such as yours . . . well . . . it wouldn't be right. What's the difference, anyway? God lends to his creations the power to make creations of their own. To build a lute is an act of creation in the purely physical sense. To make music with that lute is likewise an act of creation, only in a higher sense. No, Margaret, I'm not displeased. You've made a good decision."

She embraced and kissed her father.

"And now," he said, arising, "just give me your opinion of that Hieber over there, and tell me if you don't agree that it's twice as good as Mr. Johnson, amateur musician, is pledged to pay me for it."

"You're a modern Stradivarius ," she said, as she took the instrument from its hanging-place and sat herself upon a low stool close at hand. There she plucked the open strings and delicately plied its tuning pegs, her ear turned attentively toward the soundboard of the lute. She made a skillful assay of the scales, stopped to adjust the position of a single fret, then suddenly broke forth into *Mistress Winter's Jump*, a merry jig, both simple to play and joyful to hear.

Then, in a trice, a different lute was in her hands, and everything was changed.

The place was not the same, nor was the time. Three people sat before him playing lutes, within a spacious room, accoutered in a rustic style. Within a massive hearth, a well-stoked fire burned. The trio he beheld comprised the luthier, his daughter, and a woman of the same age as the man, no doubt his wife. Father and daughter appeared to have aged before his eyes, for now the man seemed stockier in build, his hair thinner and streaked with tones of gray, while the girl, though beautiful indeed, had lost the bloom and freshness of her youth. She seemed to counterfeit, in younger type, the form and features of the older woman, playing near her on a descant lute, her whole attention focused on the music she addressed. Reading from a different source, the fingers of the gentleman both plucked and stopped the many strings arrayed upon a long-necked lute, a chittarone by name. The younger woman played a tenor lute, and the trio of tenor, bass and descant made a beautiful rendition of *Canzone a Tre Liuti,* offspring of the seventeenth-century Italian composer Alessandro Piccinini. And it was no less lovely for the means by which it came to Aaron's sense — not directly to his brain by way of ear, but by some strange effect involving neither brain nor ear.

The spacious room in which he stood unseen was comfortably appointed, and decked out warmly in the bright and cheerful trappings of the Christmas holiday. Its central focus was a wooden crèche, with wooden figures, artfully designed with fascinating craft and careful fealty to nuance in its every detail. No tiny manger scene was this, to set within a corner as an afterthought. The Holy Family had been carved with loving care, as had the shepherds, and the Magi, and the angels floating overhead, each depicted playing on a lute, the verisimilitude of which gave ample testimony as to who their maker might have been. The edifice itself was a pavilion, open on all sides. It stood before a large fixed window, outside of which a raging blizzard blew, with moaning winds and driven snow, obscuring sight of everything beyond.

"There!" exclaimed the man, upon conclusion of the piece. "Absolutely perfect! We couldn't possibly have done it better! Piccinini would be proud!"

The younger woman smiled, a qualifying sparkle in her eye.

"It was good," she said.

"You musicians!" scoffed the man, though he was grinning all the while. "Never satisfied! Pedantic to a fault!" He laughed.

"*I* call it virtuosity," she laughed in turn.

"Perhaps," her father mused, and placed the chittarone upon a stand nearby. "Pedantry waits on virtuosity, I think. But I'm not one to talk." He rose and walked toward the crèche, and stood in thoughtful reverie before his work. He lingered momentarily, then stopped to contemplate the scenery outside.

"Just look at it," he mused. "Beautiful, yet frightening."

"We're going to be snowed right in," the older woman said, in dire tones.

"Who cares?" the man replied, still gazing at the snow. "We're snug enough in here. We've plenty of firewood, and candles, and provisions. Terrible as this wind is, I don't think it's going to blow the roof off any time soon." He turned back from the window, revealing as he did a face grown red and flushed.

"How strange you look!" observed his wife. And this was echoed by her child.

"Do I? I think I'm coming down with something. When I was out with Angus at the vet's the other day it seemed like everybody had a cold or worse. Sniff-sniff!

Cough, cough, cough! That's all I heard. Where *is* Angus? He's not outside, I hope?"

"Of course he's not," the daughter said. "He's underneath the table, sound asleep. I don't think he's feeling very well. He's been moping all day long."

"That's his age," her father laughed. "Which is just about the same with me. These joints of mine are really acting up. It's the weather . . . this cold, wet weather. Shall we have a Christmas song?" He took the tenor lute into his hands.

"Something appropriate, I believe," he said, and then began to sing.

"There is no rose of such virtue . . . ."

It wasn't a preamble, but a hint. He commenced to play a simple chordal accompaniment, while mother and daughter, as alto and soprano, passionately sang these moving words, in the two-part harmony called *fauxbourdon*.

> *There is no rose of such virtue,*
> *As is the rose that bare Jesu.*
> *Alleluia.*
>
> *For in this rose containèd was,*
> *Heaven and earth in little space.*
> *Res miranda.*

75

Blinding snow blew all about him now as Aaron stood outside, he knew not where. Upon his frame the snow and wind had no effect. And yet they chilled him in a different way, a product of some inner sense, beyond experience.

> *By that rose we may well see,*
> *That he is God in persons three.*
> *Pari forma.*

> *The angels sung the shepherds to:*
> *Gloria in excelsis deo.*
> *Gaudeamus!*

He stood inside the room again, beside the crèche. The fire in the hearth shone red and glowing on the faces of the family as they sang. What cares and troubles each had borne in mundane life he could not know, but for the time they seemed as blithe and gay and free of woe as human creatures possibly could be.

> *Leave we all this worldly mirth,*
> *And follow we this joyful birth.*
> *Transeamus.*

And even as their voices faded out, the room stood cold and dark, for now the fire in the hearth was dead.

The selfsame room, yet not the same. No change in his perspective had occurred, but even so the room was not the same. Cold, dank light illuminated all, diffusing from the window pane, reflected dully from the drifts of virgin snow. Before the hearth two silent figures lay, huddled still and silent on the floor. They were human forms.

He moved away. From time and place to time and place.

In summer sun he stood before a broad ravine. What was it he perceived, amongst the bushes and the saplings and the undergrowth that grew so thickly on its deeply sloping sides? Something out of place. Something not belonging to that quiet sylvan scene. A pile of clothes; a heap of trash, perhaps. It turned into a winter scene, and then a summer scene once more. The object changed. Thrice more the seasons came and went, disclosing finally what lay beneath the heap of rubbish at the base of the ravine. Cruel world. Cruel, hard, unfeeling world.

Drewries Accordes was in his head once more, as sight and sense returned. He looked to find himself inside the church again, playing the duet, as if nothing had transpired since the time of his departure.

X.

"My God!" he spoke distractedly, as one emerging from a swoon. "My God . . . my God." He closed his eyes and shook his head, as if he would have cast aside and rid himself of something that had lit upon it. Opening them once again he saw his spectral friend, appealing in her beauty; haloed in her own soft light.

"I . . . I have been . . ." he stammered.

"I know," he heard her say, in soothing tones. "Don't try to give it speech. There are no words for it."

"Where have I been?" he asked. "In . . . in the other world?"

"No," was her reply, "not in the *other* world, for there is only one, which springs forth from that Meaning giving birth to all. But think no more of it. You'll understand, in time."

Aaron looked about. Nothing in the scope of what he saw had changed, except a single thing. Behind her on the altar, visible within the spirit's light, appeared the crèche that he had seen inside the house, with all its figures placed as he had seen them in their former state.

"Those people . . ." he began. "I know them now. I didn't recognize them then . . . how *couldn't* I have recognized them then? It seemed as if I did, and yet my thoughts were very strange, and hardly thoughts at all. That man I saw . . . he was your father. The woman was your mother. The ones who played for me inside my house."

"They were," she said.

"And their daughter . . . was you."

"She was."

"And shortly afterward, you died."

"We died, all three." And as she spoke, her light grew dim, and flickered for an instant, like a candle's flame.

"Tell me please what happened there," he pled.

"Play," was her reply, "and I will speak. Play."

Doing as she bade, he played by rote, beginning with *Pavana Bray*, a quaint and placid dance that barely resonated in that quiet place, so lightly did he touch the strings. And as he played, she spoke, although her words, unlike his notes, suffused his mind by some means other than the agency of sound.

"We passed that Christmas quietly at home. I was working, and the holidays were free. The blizzard caught us by surprise, but we were hardly unprepared, living in rough country as we did. Our Christmas was a happy one. But late that night our dog fell ill and died. Father was sick by late next afternoon, and frighteningly so. Mother, too, grew ill. Both were weak and feverish. We huddled in the music room, as we were wont to call it, near the fireplace, our only source of heat. Meanwhile, all that day it snowed as I had never seen it snow before. Father and Mother grew progressively worse, until both were delirious with fever, and lapsing in and out of consciousness.

Father's hands were turning black, a sure sign of gangrene, and I felt horrified to think that he would lose his hands, and with those hands his livelihood as well. I nursed them both as best I could, but it seemed clear to me that they would die unless assistance could be had. But how could it be had? Help was several miles away; there was no way to call for it, and even then, the few roads leading to our house were absolutely blocked with snow. It was a dire situation, that led me to a hopeless and a desperate resolve."

Music flowed from Aaron's lute, as solemnly he gazed into her eyes and listened awestruck to the words he could not hear, yet nonetheless perceived.

"If no help reached them, they would surely die. I reasoned that the best thing, which was hardly anything at all, would be to walk, through driven snow and brutal wind, and reach the town below. You have witnessed the result. It could not have ended other than it did. Disoriented; mad with cold; weak from exhaustion and the sickness that by then had come upon me, I wandered far out of my way, and fell into a deep ravine, where lay those fragments of the earthly thing that once I was. My corpse was never found."

Aaron ceased to play, and silence hovered over all.

"But why," asked Aaron, "do you tell me this?"

"Patience!" cried the ghost. "Play again, and I will tell you more. How masterfully you play! There is something

80

in your music that vitalizes and refreshes me! I suffered greatly there, in that ravine, my body racked with pain so all-pervading that it seized my mind and made me insensible to every other thought than of the misery that I endured. I grew numb, at last, and lapsed into unconsciousness. Presently I was in a different place, seeing without eyes, hearing without ears, and knowing without thought. There were no concerns for that which I had left behind, and no regrets that I could feel, for feeling and emotion both were gone, supplanted by perceptions far beyond the ones I had experienced in life. Though born into a new and different world, I yet retained my knowledge of the old. I understood as well that I was now in bliss, although the means of feeling it had been replaced — by something else so past the realm of feeling as to beggar human reason. Trust me, Aaron. Have faith in what I say."

"I will!" cried Aaron, as he ceased to play once more. "Beautiful spirit, you have something to relate to me, of that I'm sure! Can't you tell it to me in so many words, or must you be mysterious, and speak to me in riddles?"

"Play along with me," she said, "and I will show you more."

As if by one consent they once again broke into a duet. *Twenty Ways Upon the Bells* they played, and as before, he found himself upon the sudden in another place, but this time one that he had seen in days gone by.

XI.

"MARLEY!"

The admonition came too late. A long-haired sheep-dog bounded from the steps of a gazebo, where resting it had kept its watch above a pleasant arbor, overhung with green and growing vines. Its attention had been drawn toward a fledgling robin, just emerged from cover. The baby bird had not a chance, or so one would have thought. Bounding forth in long and fluid strides, the dog stopped short, lowered its nose, and gently kissed and nudged the tiny creature as it flapped its shaky wings and hopped into the cover of a nearby bush, safe for then from all marauding beasts of prey. The Sheltie turned about, and with his long tail waving like a plume, jogged proudly back to greet his waiting lord, who seized him by the ruff and praised him to the skies.

"That's my Marley! That's my toonie-dog! Aaron!" he called aloud to someone standing in the shadows with a rake in hand. "Did you see that?"

"I did," said Aaron, as forth he stepped into the light. "He's a beautiful and gentle dog. I doubt that he could harm a flea."

"That's his nature," said Reverend Honeybutter, for it was the minister himself, though in a younger form. "A perfect shepherd, whose only care in life is for his flock. Even if his flock is just a baby bird."

"Much as you, yourself," was the reply.

Strange it was for Aaron now to see himself, as others might have seen him, in the flesh, in all dimensions, in a younger form. He understood the time and place, for he had moved within them at a certain point in his life. He watched the drama playing out before his spirit eyes as though it were a film, projected on a screen, even though the sense of its reality was strong and undeniable.

The pastor smiled and looked abashed. "You think so, Aaron?" he inquired, as all the while he stroked the dog about its thick, lush mane. "Put that rake down for a bit . . . you work too hard, you know; harder than anyone I've ever seen. Take a break for once! I've got something to confide in you. Aaron, I'm a heretic."

It was Aaron's turn to smile.

"It's odd that you should place your confidence in me," he said. "You never asked about my past before you took me on. Would it interest you to know that I'm an educated man . . . at least on parchment?"

"I suspected that," the minister replied. "I could tell it by the way you speak, and how you hold yourself."

"Could you have guessed to what extent?"

"No, and on that score I wasn't too concerned. What about it? Just how educated *are* you, Aaron?"

"Well, Reverend . . . ." he began.

"Call me Basil," said the minister. "That's my name, and I like it better than the stuffy term that sets me on a pedestal I'd rather not be on. It's Greek, you know." He winked.

"That I *do* know," Aaron said. "As for education, I've a bachelor's degree in music performance . . . classical guitar . . . and a doctorate in theology. You see," he carried on, "I've always been obsessed with certain things; ideas if you will. I couldn't let them rest. I suppose you could say I pursued them to extremes. And though my degrees, perhaps, are useless, the insight and the knowledge I accrued from getting them I think were of more worth than any credential I might have taken to the marketplace to sell."

As he watched and listened, Aaron — the spirit Aaron if you will, and not the corporeal one — grew conscious of another presence in the garden. A dark-haired girl, with book in hand, emerged upon the flagstone walkway leading from the house, and entered the gazebo, obscured from sight (but not *his* sight) behind a drapery of leaves and vines. Opening her book, she unselfconsciously began to sing.

A Fantasia for Two Lutes

Thou mighty God, that rightest every wrong,
Listen to Patience, in a dying song.

"There's more to life than money," said the minister.

"Yes. Yes, that's true. More to life than money," murmured Aaron. He briefly looked askance, as if absorbed in thought.

When Job had lost his children, lands and goods,
Patience assuagèd his excessive pain,
And when his sorrows came as fast as floods,
Hope kept his heart, till comfort came again.

"Though I'm hardly the person to profess it, seeing that I've been blessed with money, through no great effort of my own. My father was a shrewd and enterprising man. He left me and my sisters with comfortable means; enough so that we might never have to work, if we were frugal, and not too materialistic. I own the grounds here, and the church itself, and all the donations go to support *them*, and those other things that fall under the heading of pious works. For me it's idyllic. My needs aren't great. I love the old churchyard, and the church that's in it, and the house and grounds. I really get a kick out of cultivating these vines, and making wine out of the grapes; gallons of it, that I end up having to give away, because there's more of it than I could ever use myself. I love my garden, and all the work involved with it. I love the history of the place. In brief, Aaron, I think what I'm saying is that I'm content with what I've got, and not ashamed of how I got it."

"You seem to have found here," said Aaron, "what I most desire. Peace of mind. Equanimity. Passing one's days in honest work, and quiet contemplation. Not quite a monastic way of life, but almost. I think," he stated, pausing for a trice, "I might as soon have been a monk. Except . . . ." There followed yet another pause.

"No need to say it," spoke the minister. "It's the celibacy, eh?"

"Oh no!" cried Aaron, with a laugh. "Not that at all! Quite the opposite, really. I'm not married, and I've no intention of ever being married. No, it's the dogma. I've spent too much time reflecting to accept that part of it uncritically. And without uncritical acceptance, there's just no way — no *honest* way — to live that sort of life. Which is also why, Basil, if you'll pardon me for saying it . . . I'm not a Christian."

When David's life by Saul was often sought,
And worlds of woes did compass him about,
On dire revenge he never had a thought,
But in his griefs, Hope still did help him out.

"And I suppose you think," returned the minister, "that I'm to be appalled by your admitting it? Aaron! You've worked for me, what is it, two years now? I think I'm a good enough judge of character to know that you're a good man; kind and gentle like my handsome Marley here; a man given over to study, and reflection, and complete self-abnegation. You tell me you're not a Christian. Well! You certainly behave like one! Do you believe in God?"

"I believe in God," was the reply.

"Nothing else?"

"I believe in the Commandments, as they were handed down to Moses. I believe that they are precious gifts to us, and not simply the means by which God tests our loyalty to Him. I believe in the Golden Rule, as spoken by Hillel, and particularly his saying of it 'that is the whole Torah; the rest is commentary.' Regarding which I can't help but think, give me the Torah, Rabbi, and keep the commentary — that is, the dogma — for yourself."

He spoke the words with unusual force for one of his placid disposition.

"Let's at least have *some* of it," the minister replied, "lest I find myself without a job!" He smiled broadly as he said this; broadly and good-naturedly. His eyes smiled, too.

"You claimed just now to be a heretic," the young man

87

said. "I think you were about to explain yourself when the subject changed."

"Yes I was, indeed," came the reply. "And for a brief while I thought I oughtn't have brought it up at all. However, I suspected you were a man I could confide in. Now I have no doubt of it. Aaron, you've admitted that you're not a Christian. Let me make an admission of my own. I'm hardly one myself."

When the poor Cripple by the pool did lie,
Full many years in misery and pain,
No sooner he on Christ had set his eye,
But he was well, and comfort came again.

"Nominally, I'm a minister of the Christian faith," he said, giving a furtive look askance, as if he feared that other ears might be attuned. "I'm supposed to be a preacher of the Gospel . . . but you know, Aaron, this isn't the Middle Ages, when people were illiterate, and overworked, and hardly had the time of day for anything apart from what it took to keep them living, hand-to-mouth. My flock, if you want to call it that, are all intelligent people, who don't require preaching to. What they want, actually, is an establishment that represents a solid authority behind their system of belief; something that lends it credence. They want someone to lead them in their prayers, and preside over their baptisms, and their marriages, and their deaths. There's an element of magic, too . . . something primal, deeply seated in the human mind. It's the sense that somehow my ordination makes me closer to God than they are themselves, and that His power flows through me."

"A hoary superstition," offered Aaron, as he wryly smiled. "But indispensible to faith — Christian or otherwise."

"And I don't deny it them. What harm is in it? But we can't all take comfort in such things. Some of us are given to thought . . . I amongst them. I did a lot of thinking in my younger days. Perhaps it would have been better if I'd kept with my studies, and let other people do the thinking for me. But, well, I was always a rebellious sort, and so I thought . . . and thought, and thought some more. At last I came to the conclusion that most of what I'd been taught until that point was misguided, even wrong. And would you like to know exactly what my greatest conflict was? Don't faint! My greatest point of conflict was the concept of a God made manifest as Man."

"Really!" interjected Aaron, as if he were genuinely surprised.

"Yes, really. My intellect recoiled from the notion, even though it was the essence of what I was, and the calling I had answered."

89

"It must have preyed upon your mind," said Aaron.

"It did," replied the pastor. "More than I can ever say, and more than you can ever know. I loved the Christian faith, but found as I went on that there were things about that faith which strained credulity . . . mostly concepts that were laid upon it by philosophers attempting to square dogma with dogma, until at last nothing of its original intent remained, and all of it was dogma, believed because the dogma by that time had turned into the very crux of what it was. I won't bore you with the details. Perhaps we can discuss it at length some other time, or times, if you'd like."

"I would," said Aaron, quietly. "But how — if ever — were you reconciled?"

"I had a dream," was the reply. "I dreamt that I was God."

No David, Job, nor Cripple in more grief.
Christ grant me patience and my Hopes relief.

"That you were God," repeated Aaron, when the pause of half a minute had elapsed.

"Aaron, I'm not God," affirmed the minister. "I knew it even in the dream, though it seemed real, as real to my sleeping senses as the reality of our being here in the very midst of what we *know* is not a dream. I take no stock in dreams. They're nothing more than Freud said they were: the playing out in dramatic and symbolic form our frustrated impulses and desires. But the dream . . . it made me think, and led me finally to conclude that what Christ attributed to himself he was really ascribing to us all."

Silence followed once again, though shorter than the pause that had preceded it.

"He spoke in parables," said Aaron, his eyes cast down, as if in pensive thought. Nor did he raise them, as the elder man continued with his discourse.

"In parables. Yes, in parables; how could he have spoken otherwise? His were revolutionary thoughts; far too revolutionary for the times; for *any* times. He spoke of himself as the son of God. In later years, philosophers turned him *into* God. And killed each other over whether it was God since the beginning of time, or from some point after the event. Good Christians, eh? I told myself, if He were God, then *we* are God as well. And we are most decidedly *not*! But then . . . and be patient with me, Aaron . . . I chanced to come upon an odd remark, by a certain famous author, who arguing a point said, 'what you do not own, not even God may take away from you.' Have you any idea what that suggests?"

Aaron pondered for a moment.

"That God," he said at last, "is not omnipotent."

"You are either extremely perceptive," replied the minister, as his face appeared to glow, "or I'm not as mad as some might think. Maybe both! Hear me out, though, Aaron, and I'll make an end of this. His presence gives substance to the universe. Being all spirit, He has no eyes to see; no ears to hear; no tactile sense to experience the things of His creation, as they exist in time and space. But *we*, His sapient creations; *we* possess those things, as well as the intelligence to explore and learn through them. Suppose *we* are the agency by which He lives and moves within the world, and understands the details of the thing that He has wrought? And what greater love than that He should share our pain and pleasure, through the medium of our senses? To live and love with us, and suffer with us too? Not just in one life, but in untold millions of them, from the lowest to the most exalted? What say you, Aaron? Am I insane? Am I a heretic?"

No David, Job, nor Cripple in more grief.
Christ grant me patience and my Hopes relief.

"Not a madman," Aaron said. "But yes . . . a heretic."

His state of agitation at an end, the pastor grinned, and placed his hand on Aaron's shoulder.

"I trust you won't expose me," he implored.

"I most certainly will not."

"Thanks. Thanks for letting me get it off my back. We needn't talk about it any more."

"I'll ponder what you've told me," Aaron said, and turned about as if he would depart. The pastor stopped him.

"You know, I find it strange," he said, "that you of all people haven't contradicted me. I expected it. Do you mind if I make a personal observation?"

"Not at all," was the reply.

"There's something about you that seems inexpressibly sad. You laugh and smile; you throw yourself into your work with all your heart and soul, and do it cheerfully as well. You're quiet and stoic, and completely uncomplaining. Yet something is bothering you. If you'd ever like to share it with me, I'd be more than willing to listen, and maybe lend a hand, if I can help."

"Thanks," said Aaron, as he turned to go. He gave the minister a friendly smile, and it was warmly given back. They shook hands. And so they parted.

He wondered now why he had drifted there, to look upon a scene whose details he remembered well, despite the lapse of many years. Yet as he watched — still floating in the aura of that ghostly sense to which he now was used

— and as the figures of the men diverged, he noted something he could not have seen when first it had occurred. Melissa rose, her book in hand, and stepped into the garden. From there she stood and watched him as he walked toward the graveyard, never looking back.

Nor did she take her eyes away, not even when he vanished from her sight, but stood there looking wistful and forlorn, as if she pined for something which she knew, for all the world, that she would never, ever come to call her own.

XII.

HE LOOKED INTO those eyes, and they were nearer than before. She sat inside the chapel, in the corner where the organ stood. She sat upon its bench with a guitar in hand, while on the bench in front of her a book of music lay. Aaron's younger self had passed into the church, carrying a bucket and a mop. He watched her as she swept the book aside, and stamped her foot upon the floor.

"I give up!" Melissa cried, and looked toward the rafters of the nave. Lowering her eyes, she saw him in the aisle, and smiled abashedly.

"Why do you give up?" he called, his voice echoing across the empty space. "What exactly are you trying to do?" Coming next to her and reaching down, he gathered up the book of music that she had in her impatience cast aside.

"This is lute music," he observed, thumbing through its pages while furtively eying her countenance as it blushed a rosy shade of red. "A tutorial, to be precise. Are you studying the lute?"

She rolled her pretty eyes.

"Not quite," was her reply. "It's nothing, really . . . just playing around."

"Is that your lute?" he asked, and gave a nod at the guitar she held, a classical guitar.

"It's my *guitar*, the tuning of which I've modified to imitate the lute."

"You sound upset," he said.

"I'm not upset," she sighed. "I'm simply disgusted with myself and my lack of progress. And it's not for want of trying! I'm not exactly stupid when it comes to music. I mean, goodness, I *teach* the flute, and several other instruments as well! When *you* play it sounds so beautiful; so appealing, that I thought . . . do I have to say it? But I give up. It simply isn't working out. Maybe I'm lazy. Maybe I haven't got the aptitude."

Taking the guitar, he plucked the open strings. "Very good," he softly said, and gave it back to her.

"Play something," he suggested. "Something easy, that you've played before."

"On this?" she said. "No, thank you, sir; not in front of you. I'd be ashamed!"

"Do you think I'd laugh at you?"

"Inwardly, perhaps." She spoke the words demurely.

"You say you teach."

"I do," was her reply.

"And do you laugh, inwardly or otherwise, when your pupils make mistakes?"

"No," she bashfully replied, as she cast her dark eyes down, and gently shook her head.

"Here's a simple piece," said Aaron, looking through the book. "*Mr. Dowland's Midnight*, by who else? Come on now, Melissa, don't be shy!" He placed the book before her, on the bench.

And so, with a great show of reluctance, she played. But she did it badly; so very badly that the piece was out of rhythm, with many discordant sounds, and false notes competing with the muted ones.

"That was terrible," she said, when she had finished, and an awkward silence had ensued.

"I don't know," he soothed. "There were some promising aspects to it."

"Oh spare me!" she cried. "It was awful, and you know

it! Promising aspects indeed!" But she didn't sound displeased, or out-of-sorts, for she regarded Aaron with a pert and naughty grin, and never took her eyes from his the while.

"Have you got a tutor?" he inquired.

"No," she said, "I was waiting to give it a try on my own and see if it would be worthwhile pursuing, which of course it's not. I want ability. Better I devote my time to what I have a talent for, than wasting it on something that will never be."

She looked wistful now, though whether it was for the wasted time, or something altogether else, the watching shade of Aaron could not tell. He recollected having lived through this event, just as he recalled his meeting with the minister. But why he should have come back to revisit those events remained a mystery.

"However, I was wondering if, perhaps . . . ." She brightened suddenly and gave a look of hope. Just as suddenly, a cloud came over her.

"Wondering?" prompted Aaron. "Wondering . . . ."

"Oh, nothing," she replied. "That is, only that tomorrow is Christmas, and I was hoping you might come visit us. Bring your lute, perhaps, and play."

"Perhaps," was his reply.

"You won't, will you?" she asked, although she said it in a way that showed her perfectly resigned.

"Perhaps," he said again.

"Will you play for me now?"

"On *that*?" he queried, nodding his head at the guitar.

"Yes, on that, if you don't mind. *Mignarda*, if you please."

And so he did as he was asked, rendering the tune upon her old guitar, as nicely and enchantingly as if it were the finest representative of its kind. A slow, sad and moving piece he played, and as he played, Melissa softly sang the words that had been written to its melody.

> *Shall I strive with words to move,*
> *When deeds receive not due regard?*
> *Shall I speak, and neither please,*
> *Nor be freely heard?*
>
> *Grief, alas, though all in vain,*
> *Her restless anguish must reveal,*
> *She alone my wound shall know,*
> *Though she will not heal.*
>
> *All woes have end, though a while delayed,*
> *Our patience proving,*

A Fantasia for Two Lutes

Oh, that Time's strange effects,
Could but make her loving!

Storms calm at last,
And why may not she,
Leave off her frowning?

Oh, sweet Love,
Help her hands,
My affection crowning.

I woo'ed her; I loved her,
And none but her admire.
Oh come, dear Joy,
And answer my desire!

And now, amazingly, the hands that played were his, and even more amazingly the eyes that watched were his. They gazed forth from a body that had once belonged to him, and marked the pining woman as she hovered near. And as she sang, the heartache, and the sorrow, and the fruitless yearning all contained within the song were carried in her visage, and her voice.

Then, wonderful to say, his other self was gone, and she

was gone as well. A pair of eyes gazed into his. But they were not Melissa's eyes.

A loud peal sounded from the organ, as the black man on the sudden turned and struck its keys. He played a gaudy flourish, then he stopped, and turned again, and laughed aloud.

"A-ha-ha-ha! A-ha-ha-ha-ha-ha!"

He turned again toward the keyboard and he played another flourish. Then back he turned, and laughed again; the same laugh as before.

"A-ha-ha-ha! A-ha-ha-ha-ha-ha!"

Then suddenly his mood grew serious. "Are you a fool?" he asked. "Or are you simply blind?"

"I don't know what you mean," was the reply. At which the black man groaned.

"Both!" he cried, triumphantly. "Both!"

"Enlighten me," said Aaron. "Wherein am I blind? In what way have I played the fool?"

"You have the nerve to ask? Is that your lute?" He spoke the words sarcastically, and turned his head toward the old guitar, propped up against the balustrades.

"You know what it is," replied Aaron, indignantly. "And it's not mine, it's Melissa's."

"That girl!" the black man cried. "That poor, sweet, *suffering*, pretty girl, with those big, soft eyes and milk-white skin, and rosy cheeks! You know her, Aaron, dear. The one who dotes on you." His tone grew confidential. "Lives for you. Dwells upon your every word and every glimpse of you. Will be a spinster maid for you. Ah, *so* much love to give, and *such* a man for her to squander it upon! Don't tell me that it's so! Don't say it! There's no need to confirm it, man! Because I'm *right*, and it's so *obvious*!"

"I don't care for her," said Aaron. His voice was low, emotionless and flat.

"Don't lie!" cried Mr. Indigo. "Don't lie!" He shook his finger, chidingly. "Don't lie to me! Nor to yourself! Lies are bad! Lies distort reality and make us weak of will! Embrace the truth, my friend! Isn't it true that you admire and respect her? Don't lie! I know your heart, as well as if I lived within you, body, mind and soul. Do you admit it, man?"

"I'm not indifferent to her virtues," Aaron said, and this time there was ire in his voice.

"A-*haaaaaa*!" the black man said, and drew it out with mocking emphasis. "Now we're making progress! A good beginning, Aaron, friend . . . not the best beginning, mind, but good! And so just tell me, if you'll be so kind, why you won't visit her on Christmas Day, when by that simple act alone you give her recompense for everything she's done for you?"

"You annoy me," was Aaron's curt reply.

"No doubt!" the black man said. "Or possibly you give yourself annoy. Consider, though: I neither think nor act for you. Nor do I strive to play you for a fool, as you so often do, and very well, upon yourself! By now you know that I speak only truth, and have no inclination to deceive."

"The Devil is a deceiver," Aaron said. "The wisdom of the ages bears it out."

"Do I deceive?" asked Mr. Indigo.

"What else can I think?"

"You're wrong," said Mr. Indigo.

"I am?"

"Of course!" the black man cried. "Were I to ask, I think you couldn't find a single instance where I've lied to you. Why would I even try?" He shrugged. "What possible effect could it have on you?"

"To break my faith," said Aaron, forcefully. "To break my faith, and rot the core of my belief."

"BELIEF?" the black man shrieked aloud, and held his hands imploringly aloft. "*Belief*? Oh, *why*? Why? Why should I strive to rot the core of your *belief*? Behold me, Aaron!" he appealed, as to his knees he fell, and held his hands together in a mockery of prayer. "Look into these eyes, and if you never trusted me before, be sure of this as you are sure of life itself! I charge you now: *Believe! Believe!* With all your heart: *Believe!* With all your soul: *Believe!* With all the strength and power you command: *Believe, believe, believe!* Cherish your belief! And never let it lapse! *Believe!*"

Up from his knees he rose, and Aaron looked upon that form, not by the light that shone within the church, but by the selfsame light outside its doors, within the cemetery close at hand. They stood before a pair of graves. Not any graves, but two specific graves amongst the rest. Upon the single gravestone was the name of BOARD.

The black man drew up close, and lightly placed his hand on Aaron's arm.

"Believe," he softly said. And having said the word, he disappeared.

XIII.

I pray thee, watch my cows for me,
Carillo, wilt thou? Tell.
First let me have a kiss of thee,
And I will watch them well.

OR MAYBE IT was Aaron who had disappeared, for Margaret sat beside him once again, as he played for her the simple yet beguiling tune of *Guardame las Vacas*, a theme by

Narvaez, with seven *diferencias*, the notes of each more deftly interwoven than the one before. What sounded to the ear the essence of simplicity, assumed within the mind a clear impression of the opposite.

"I love that piece," the spectre softly said, and there was sadness in her tone. "Only one thing would give me greater pleasure than to hear it as you've played it to me now."

"And what is that?" he asked.

"To hear it as you do, with human ears, connected to a mortal mind."

"Can't you hear it, then?"

"Yes," she sighed, "in my own way. But not in *your* way. Oftentimes we spirits yearn for little aspects of the world we left behind — a world of feeling and a sense of oneness with the physical Creation. Not an emotional pining, such as you of flesh and blood might know; not a frustrated desire for action that gnaws upon your mortal bowels. It is a quiet, peaceful longing that draws the spirit back toward the world he left behind; toward the beauty and the mystery of the universe, and to the rapture of living as part of that universe, even with the change and turbulence that wait upon it."

"In all of my philosophy," Aaron mused, "I never would have thought it so."

"You doubt it?" asked the ghost.

"No; no," was his reply. "It isn't that. It's only that I have, through your intercession, been given an understanding, however slight, of the world that you inhabit. Who, if the choice were his, would ever wish a return to the pain, uncertainty and fear of mortal life?"

"You've had a foretaste of my world. Do not presume," she said, "that you have experienced the full measure of existence in that world. You speak as a child who is ignorant of the alterations that must come upon him as his life proceeds. Do you recall this little verse?

> "When I am grown to man's estate,
> I shall be very proud and great,
> And tell the other girls and boys,
> Not to meddle with my toys."

Her blue eyes sparkled in her own peculiar light, as Aaron laughed aloud to hear the verse of Stevenson, so very brief and poignant, with universal wisdom in its four short lines. He then fell sober once again.

"Tell me, then, why this must be," he said at last. "Are you bored?"

"No. It's not within my nature."

"Are you compelled against your will?"

"No. My will is mine and mine alone."

"Why, then? Why?" he pled.

"There are people in this world of yours," she answered him, "incapable of feeling fear. Of *feeling* fear," she emphasized. "But not of understanding all the dangers fear must place them on their guard against. Like them, I have no feeling, but I somehow have remembrance . . . remembrance of the world in which I lived, and what existence was within that world. To see. To hear. To touch. To feel my weight as it was drawn toward the earth, reminded always that the substance of my being sprang therefrom."

"To feel suffering and pain," mused Aaron quietly.

"Transitory!" cried the ghost. "Of brief duration in the span of human life, when set against the endlessness of broad eternity! The necessary cost of having lived that life and known the pleasures mortal life affords! Oh, to be alive once more! And come back to this peaceful place again to rest from life, and be renewed!"

"And would you have it so?"

"If it were in my power . . . yes."

He paused, and seemed to lose himself in thought. He tried to speak, in vain. At last the spirit spoke.

"Aaron, play your lute," she bade. "Something very simple . . . the simplest piece you know."

And so he played that piece. And though it was a simple piece indeed, he played it with a feeling so intense that its simplicity was overshadowed by the skill with which he gave it life.

"*Pavana de Alexandre*," he declared, with a smile.

"Alonso de Mudarra," she replied. "A consummate musician, and a master of the Spanish lute. A simple piece, indeed. The cornerstone of beauty is simplicity."

"I played that piece for many years before I owned a lute, or even thought of lutes apart from paintings where the angels played them in celestial scenes. Yes, it's beautiful. As much so as this instrument I've played it on." He turned the lute face-up, regarding it with wonderment and awe.

"Though it has," the spirit said, "no voice of its own."

"No voice?" Aaron cried. "And yet it sings!"

She smiled and gently shook her head.

"It has no voice of its own," she said again. "Devoid of your touch, it has no life. Yours is the animating force that makes it sing, and sing so beautifully. Your spirit enters it, imbuing it with powers that exceed the limits of its nature. There is a class of things which men call instruments, by which they work their wills upon the world. The lute is of a special class of instrument, by which men's minds reach out and speak to other men in ways that words alone cannot. Do you understand?"

"I think I understand."

"And understand that while the lute is dumb and life-less in and of itself, each human mind has been imbued with freedom, will and memory?"

"Yes! Yes!" he cried. "That is to say, I understand your words themselves. But can you see how hard it is for mortal minds to grasp the mysteries of things so far beyond their ken?"

"I can, for I was mortal . . . in my time."

"What is it that you mean to tell me, or relate to me?"

"Neither to tell, nor to relate," the ghost replied, "but rather, to reveal." She slightly turned toward the crèche, whose figures now shone brighter in her light. "Christmas is upon us," she observed. "Behold the Magi, and the gifts they bear. I bear a gift for you, which rises up from my immortal will, and comes to being through a power granted to me from the wellspring of all power."

"I am blessed," said Aaron in reply. "Your presence here, alone, is as a precious gift to me."

"And will you have it of me?" she inquired, "trusting that I mean you only good?"

"I will have it of you, come what may." His mien was forceful, yet his voice calm. "But I cannot believe," he quickly said, "that anything which springs from you can be intended for the ill, or for that matter, come to it."

She raised her lute and struck a chord. "Play along with me," she said, "and journey once again."

Once again he followed her. Even from the outset, Aaron knew that he was slipping from the universe of sense. He felt his fingers dancing on the strings, as skillfully they moved from fret to fret. Yet no vibration of those pliant strings resounded in his ears, as from the lutes arose a duet version of the famous *Greensleeves,* quick and lively in the execution, with many variations on its simple melody. Supplanted by awareness he could never have explained, his human sense dissolved into a world of clarity, and Aaron hovered like a cloud, above a scene that he remembered all too well.

XIV.

"WOLF?"

Wolf it was indeed: alive, and young, and standing in the doorway looking stunned.

"What are you doing here?" he asked.

"I came to tell you that I got a job."

"A *job*?" He said it in a mocking tone of voice, as if the very notion seemed absurd beyond belief. "A *job* in Straffen? Doing what?"

"Plastic extrusion."

"Is that why you got a doctorate in whatever it is you studied? What exactly *did* you study, Mr. Westwode? Oh, *pardon* me, I should say *Doctor* Westwode. You *are* a doctor, aren't you? Maybe you can fix this pain I've got, right *here*."

He grimaced, then he gestured, most expressively.

"It's only just for now," the young man said, with just a hint of ire in his voice.

"Oh sure," sneered Wolf, and waved his hand dismissively. "Not to worry, though: you're smart. You'll be a supervisor in a year or so. Then you can really use that music and philosophy you squandered all that money on. What's plastic without music? What's extrusion *sans* philosophy? You're empty-handed. Did you get the shotgun shells?"

His voice was wry and full of bitter irony, even when allied with laughter. The brothers stood inside a screened-in porch, at the threshold of a small, gray house, on a dank and drizzling Christmas Eve, more than fifteen years in Aaron's past. The man who stood before his younger self was not the beaten, haggard wreck that he had last beheld, but a healthy, handsome man of thirty years, of lean form and modest stature, who stood regarding him as he had done so since their youth, with a bemused and condescending air.

"No, Wolf," was Aaron's diffident reply. "No, I didn't

get them. I need to tell you something." His eyes were downcast; his voice scarcely audible. "Not *tell* you something, actually, for there's no *telling* you anything, but to ask you something, or, rather, to ask something of you."

"Come inside the house," Wolf said.

They went inside. His hovering shadow moved along with them, though not on legs of flesh, but in the strange and drifting motion that propelled him somehow, through the wood and brick, into a long and narrow room, dark with gloom and feeble light.

Though fashioned as a living room, this space contained no furniture, except a tattered davenport, its cushions stained and threadbare. Three walls of the room were lined with wire shelving of a heavy gauge. Upon this shelving stood an odd concatenation of metallic cages, housing a menagerie of small, warm-blooded creatures. Mice and rats he saw imprisoned there, but also chipmunks, rabbits, and a solitary squirrel, wretched in appearance, as if from pining for the freedom it had lost.

"It smells in here," the younger Aaron said. He waved his hand before his face. "And why the animals? I thought you'd given up that sort of thing."

"I gave up academia, not the spirit of curiosity that inspired me to join it in the first place. Furthermore, I'm still a scientist, though you may call me mad." He grinned as he related this, a mocking smile in which a sneer could almost be discerned.

"Very well. But why the animals?"

"If you're worried about their welfare, you silly, tender-hearted fool, I mean to let them go, and soon enough."

"That's good. And what are you doing to them?"

"Just watching them."

"Why?"

"I can't tell you . . . not now, at least. Trust me, kid, it's nothing sinister or bad. At some point I'll let you in on it, but at least for now I hardly know myself. It's only an idea; a glimmer of a thought. Trust me."

"I trust you, Wolf," he said, and Wolf replied, "I know you do." And it seemed for just a moment that the sneer had left his face, and that this time he was honestly sincere.

"Wolf," spoke Aaron, after a little silence, "I told you I wanted to tell you something. No more bombs, Wolf. No more bombs. It just won't do."

He watched his brother's countenance grow dark. "You won't help me, then?" he asked.

"I won't," said Aaron flatly. "I don't understand . . . perhaps I never understood . . . what you . . . what *we* . . . are trying to accomplish. A man is hurt, and he is maimed, perhaps for life. It isn't right. You can't do such things; no

one has the right to do such things. I won't let you, Wolf."
He seemed determined; forceful even.

Wolf laughed.

"Are you kidding me?" he asked. The alteration in his mood, from dark to light within an instant's span, was very clear to see. "Surely you can see those puny firecrackers for the jokes they were!"

His face went dark a second time. He rolled his eyes toward the ceiling, held them there, then brought them down again. "Or perhaps you weren't aware? But how can that possibly be? You helped me, after all! *You* lent me money from the dwindling remains of Ma's inheritance. *You* went out and brought back the supplies. We talked about it, didn't we? We agreed upon it, did we not?"

"You told me," said Aaron, "that no one would be hurt, and I believed you."

"Hurt?" retorted Wolf, at which he winced, as if in pain. "Rubbish! That simpleton is no more hurt than you would be if you singed your eyebrows lighting up a grill. Hurt? Don't you think I could build a better bomb than any of those toys, if that was what I had in mind? I could blow a city block to bits! God, what a woeful, sentimental piece of work you are!" Wolf was angry now. He threw himself upon the threadbare davenport and sulked.

"I won't be part of it," spoke Aaron, looking down

upon his brother as he motionlessly stared into the space beyond. "Besides, what good is it? Can it really be you think such feeble acts will make a difference in the state of things, even if it's only for the worse?"

His brother laughed out loud.

"Have you never heard," he said, emerging from his sulk, "of a man named Princip? *Gavrillo* Princip? Who in the summer of 1914 fired two shots from a pistol, and changed the world forever?" His passion was extreme.

"I know the man," said Aaron, quietly. "Know him in the historical sense, that is. Certainly you don't suppose he was aware of the effect his act would have, and the incredible chain of events those shots would set in motion?"

"What difference does it make?" shrugged Wolf. "Small things have big effects."

"Perhaps," was the reply. "But no matter what the case, I have no desire to be the agent of changes such as those, when the actions that set them in motion are the means of harm to others."

The elder brother sighed, and scrutinized the younger, as one might look with pity on a person of a weak and feeble mind.

"I knew you'd feel that way," he said. "*Feel* being the operative word, for you never *think*. I'm not upset; in fact, I'm reconciled. I've known all along it would come to this, and I'm prepared to set your mind at ease. Get on with your life, kid. Go extrude your plastic, or whatever else it is you're doing with yourself these days. I don't need you."

"It's not that I won't help."

"Your help's not needed . . . at least not right this minute. Besides, your heart's not in it."

"That's not fair to me," said Aaron, and he hung his head. "I've done my part before. You know I'll gladly do it once again, in anything that isn't positively immoral. Let it be criminal, even, if it must, so long as it's not immoral."

"Good grief, you really are a fool. Very well. I don't need you now, but in the future . . . perhaps the *near* future, I'm going to need resources. My money won't last forever, and I'm never going back to work again. Don't remonstrate, it's useless. I wasn't meant to drag out that grinding, pointless existence. I'm going to do what *I* want to do, and to hell with everything else."

"Are you really never going back to work?"

"Are you deaf? I said I wasn't, and I'm not." His words and his effect were like those of a willful child. "Have you some objection?"

"For my own part, no," said Aaron. "But don't hold it against me if I mourn for any good you might have done in your career."

"Look, don't get all sweet and sticky with me now," said

Wolf, once more with his sneering mannerism. "*Good* I might have done? What do you know about the sciences? No one works alone to accomplish anything these days. You're a cog in a machine, all your so-called 'brilliance' going into making single bricks that end up with a million other bricks in an edifice that no one understands, for there's no one in the world that has the brains to understand it. Not even *me*, and that's saying something! You're one of Wagner's Nibelungen dwarfs, tinkering and hammering away on priceless treasures for his master to enjoy. Get this, Aaron: if I'm to be an ugly dwarf, I'll be an Alberich, renouncing love for power. Let other people be the slaves! I'll have none of it."

"I understand," said Aaron, in conciliating tones. "And I don't object, if that's what makes you happy. But you *must* renounce violence, if I'm to have anything to do with you. I mean it. That's final, Wolf."

Wolf shook his head and groaned.

"I told you to trust me, didn't I? You injure me, you know, in the most agonizing way, by implying that you're loath to take me at my word."

"You never gave your word, where violence was concerned."

"Well, then," he said, as demonstratively he rolled his eyes again, "I. Renounce. Violence. Does that work for you?"

"If you're sincere, it does."

"When haven't I been sincere?"

Aaron paused.

"Aha, you see!" exclaimed his brother. "You have to stop and think about it, eh? Is it because you've never known me *not* to be sincere? What are you looking at now?"

"Only *that*," was the reply. As Aaron spoke, he nodded grimly at an object that until the present moment had escaped his eye — a scene of Christ's nativity, tucked away upon a shelf; a little knick-knack such as one might purchase in a dollar store, and use to decorate a Christmas tree.

"Ah, my crèche," said Wolf. "Do you admire it?"

"Not so much as I'm astonished by it."

"That such a thing should be in my possession?"

"Yes. But why? Why, that is, do you possess it?"

"To remind me at this 'sacred' time of year," he boasted, "of the world's stupidity. To remind me that I'm better, and wiser than the common gamut of the human race, that bend the knee to this moronic tripe. Jesus, Joseph and Mary!" He wiped his lips, as if the words had soiled them. "And you're the worst of the lot! Have you got a girlfriend yet?"

"No," said Aaron, bashfully.

"That's one thing going for you. That, and the fact you're my kid brother is enough, I suppose, to stop my having nothing more to do with you. Go on; get out of here. I'm tired of looking at you, and I need to be alone; I want to think. Get me some airline tickets if you want to be of use. Business class. Round trip. To Albuquerque."

"Is that all?"

"Yes," was the reply, curt and dismissive, "that's all. Bye." He nodded sharply at the door, and the young man left, without another word; without a remonstrance.

The elder brother watched him as he disappeared from sight. And when the last of him was seen, and the rusty hinges of the outer door had squealed, he took the little manger in his hand and mused upon it silently, with something of a pensive air, and triumph sketched upon his mocking face.

Upon its hinges squeaked another door. Footsteps sounded in a corridor and echoed in a measured tread against the cold and barren walls.

The black man stood behind him, eyeing Wolf with an expectant air. Sensing his presence, Wolf turned hastily about, the crèche still in his hand. The black man started suddenly, and drew back in alarm.

"Nervous?" Wolf inquired.

"Nonsense," Mr. Indigo replied. But still he stood where he had stopped, and still he eyed the bauble nervously.

"Does this help?" Wolf turned the object in his hand

and dropped it to the floor. And then he trod upon it, crushing it to fragments, which he scattered with his foot.

Wolf peered into the black man's eyes. They gleamed, and smiled, as eyes are said to smile. His countenance expanded in a grin. Then both men smiled, and both began to laugh. They laughed together for a little while, and afterward embraced, as if they were the best of friends, whom fate had kept asunder for a long, long time.

XV.

"I NEVER UNDERSTOOD," said Aaron, "what he wanted in New Mexico. I bought the tickets for him. And the crèche . . . the Christmas scene," he murmured, half-confusedly. "Has it changed?" He tightly closed his eyes, then opened them again and shook his head. "The figures . . . have they moved?"

"Moved?" the ghost inquired. "Or been moved?"

"Both," said Aaron, wonderingly. "Why yes, they have; it's obvious. The Virgin holds the baby to her breast, though when I saw her last she sat upright, the infant sleeping soundly in the hay. Joseph greets the king who proffers gold, and takes the present from his hands, where earlier he stood by passively with folded arms. The look upon his face is one of gratitude, with due respect for majesty. The other kings were standing; now they kneel in reverence of a higher power. The very angels now are hovering in different places — how is it that they hover? What is holding them? See how their hands have moved from fret to fret upon the lutes! Why, it's positively magic! The faces are alive, as if they had been fashioned out of living flesh and blood! Margaret! Is this the crèche that stood within the window at your parents' house?"

"It is," she smiled. "My father made it as a gift to me, the year that I was born. My father was a strong yet gentle man, sometimes overcome with sentiment, and always conscious of the mystic side of life. Need I say he was religious too? But only in his deeds, and seldom in his words. He was a great admirer of beauty, and that was manifest in all his works."

"In all his works, indeed," said Aaron, as his eyes moved from the manger, to the instrument of music that he held within his hands, and lit at last upon the perfect features of the ghost.

"You are beautiful," he said. "If I could have my will, I think that I would never leave this place, so long as you were here. I'd simply rest my eyes upon you for whatever time the universe has left."

"Do not allow yourself," she said, "to be beguiled by words. I am immaterial. What you see of me, you see within your mind alone. As for Time, don't speak of it. The word conveys no sense, except within the realm of human thought. In the world through which I move there is no Time."

"And the world in which you moved before?"

"There is no Time," the ghost declared. Her voice was firm, and unequivocal.

"Men of great renown and intellect would disagree with you," he said.

"Yes," she modestly replied. "They would."

"They would contradict you," he pursued.

"Yes," she whispered, as she turned her eyes askance. "And no better could I answer than to measure my experience against their mortal pride, their mortal erudition, and their mental sleights-of-hand."

Archly did she smile, and when she did, her light glowed brighter still, and made the darkness at its edge an even deeper shade of black. "There is no Time," she said again. "Learn that, Aaron, and your understanding will increase, and you will cease to wonder at the things that strained your mind before. Learn that Form is an illusion too, whose changes foster your belief in Time, which of all illusions is the greatest one of all."

"Would you have me disbelieve in Time?" he asked, with quiet incredulity. "I, a musician?"

"No more," she spoke, "than I would ask you to renounce the words you speak. You are mortal, and must live by the conventions of your kind. Accept them as they are in mundane life. Live with them. Enjoy them. But let your higher thoughts be moved by understanding of a higher kind."

"Tell me," Aaron questioned, "what is Beauty?"

"The rendering of Chaos into Order," she replied. "The joining of elements to fashion things the human mind perceives as Form, even though the elements themselves remain unchanged, and of a single substance. Beware!" she warned. "I tell you this in words, as poor a means of speech as dumb show ever was. And though I answer you, my answer will elude you if you weigh it by the selfsame means. Do you understand?"

"I understand," said Aaron sadly, "only that I haven't got the means to understand."

"Keep it in your heart and mind," she charged him, "and its meaning will appear to you, perceived within that part of you which never dies. Consider the lute you hold within your hands. Its voice is waves upon the air, and nothing more. Yet nonetheless it speaks to you, conveying to your heart emotions felt by other men whom you have never known."

"The things that I have seen and heard," he mused, "I

know that I have neither seen nor heard, though they have come to me as if they had been seen and heard. As for words, yours comfort me as never could . . . my brother's words."

He proffered the confession with averted gaze, as if ashamed of it.

"And yet," she said, in sterner tones than she had used before, "you offered him the whole of your allegiance."

"The whole of my allegiance," he affirmed. "The whole of it." He sadly shook his head.

"Why?" she mildly asked. "Who and what was he that you should so enslave yourself to his desires?"

As she spoke, she played. Indeed, she had been playing all along, in tones whose cadence matched the rhythm of their speech.

"It was a belief of mine. A settled belief that Wolf was better . . . wiser . . . stronger than myself in every way . . . that he was always right, and that I didn't have the power to prevail in any contest governed by the mind or will. A belief that he was somehow beyond the ordinary, and that, as such, I owed allegiance to him."

"Whence sprang this strange belief?" she asked.

"You think it strange," he said. "To me, it was as natural as the fact of my existence. I'll explain. My parents were scientists, both eminent amongst their peers. My father was a biochemist; my mother a field biologist. You can't imagine their intelligence, or the high regard in which they were held by those who moved within their spheres. Our father we hardly ever saw, for his work was his life, and he pursued it with the devotion of a man whose calling is his reason for existence. He was much older than Ma, and died, when I was twelve, of melanoma. Ma ceased to work when Wolf was born, which is to say, she ceased to work outside the home, but retained her calling as the editor of many publications, all scholarly, and highly arcane. I can't ever recollect a time when Ma wasn't in the midst of something to do with one of those periodicals. Our house was strewn with books and papers, Ma's endless correspondence, and the ceaseless tap-tap-tap of the old manual typewriter at which she sat for hours at a time. I never thought it unusual, for it was the situation into which I had been born. But take it as given that in our household knowledge and its acquisition reigned supreme, and science was the means by which it was pursued. Intelligence was the yardstick by which we were measured, and by which we gauged the worth of everyone who moved within our realm.

"Imagine, if you can, how it was for a child of middling intelligence, born into such a family, with my nearest sibling, a genius in his own right, seven years advanced from me. I won't say I'm not intelligent. I know that I'm intelligent, but not in the way *they* were; not to the *extent* they were, all three, my father, my mother and their eldest child. I knew they were disappointed in me; knew quite well that they looked down on me, and patronized me, as if I had been mentally defective and they considered it their duty to look after me, burdensome as that duty was. And it wasn't that they didn't love me . . . I believe. No, it was just that I was powerless to reach them, as they truly were.

"That I idolized my brother and placed him high upon a pedestal was perhaps because I found myself completely awed by him. Though he was older, yet he was an older *child*, and I perceived of him as close to me on that account. Intellectually I could never parley with him, though my admiration for his knowledge, and what I took to be his wisdom, were positively boundless. He knew everything, and, in the course of my development, I came to take him at his word on everything, because it seemed that he was always right. It was easier to take him at his word; to take my parents at their word, not least because I'd not the wherewithal to judge them right or wrong. Theirs was the language of Science, and I was never fluent in that tongue."

"Nor I," the spirit said, "although my knowledge now would set their kind to shame. Ignorant in their arrogance, and arrogant in their ignorance."

He nodded, and continued.

"Despite all that I forged my own identity, in something that they never would have reckoned worth their time. I found I had an aptitude for music. In my father's study, mounted on the wall, hung an old flamenco guitar, strictly ornamental, and surely never played, at least so long as I had known it to have rested there. One idle day I took it down, and from that moment I divided my existence into two distinctive parts: before and after music.

"I taught myself to play that old guitar, at first in secret, from a popular tutorial that I purchased from a music store. It was magic. I could hear the voices in the notes I played, and they spoke to me in a language no less mysterious than the discourse you have shown me here tonight. The knowledge of music, both in theory and practice, I devoured hungrily, until at last I understood that I had found the identity of which I spoke; an identity of my own.

"Of course I was discovered. Far from disapproving, Ma encouraged me. I think she knew I had no faculty for science, and that it was best for me to pursue something to the point of excellence, even if it was only music. She arranged for me to have lessons with a master, and from his tutelage I greatly profited. My aptitude was great; my agility impressive. What was more . . . far more . . . was my emotional connection with the music that I played, and an understanding of the visions which had moved the people who composed it. It lent my efforts a quality unattainable by those who played by rote alone, mechanically perfect though they might have been.

"I knew my family looked down on me, despite my native talent; despite the aptitude I showed. It was never let on, but I am sure that it was felt. They professed to be proud of my ability, and affected to boast about me, but they never could appreciate — perhaps were incapable of appreciating — the true nature of my accomplishments. It was the dexterity of my hands, and not the outpouring of my heart and soul, that won their praise. Their cold and rational minds could never have conceived the idea of something higher, and nobler, and better, being there."

"In the music," spoke the ghost.

"And beyond . . . far beyond," was his reply. "For you see, I made a discovery one day, tiny in itself, but profound in what it meant to me, and my vision of the world. Tucked away in an old trunk, amongst some scattered odds and ends that had lain in our attic untouched and unremembered, I found a book . . . a Bible. It was a small, old, Gideon Bible — old, that is, in years alone, for it looked to all appearances as if no one had ever opened it. You understand, of course, that atheism, in our household, reigned supreme. If we were certain of nothing else, we were one hundred percent certain in the nonexistence of a deity. There were not supposed to be Bibles, or Torahs, or any other work pertaining to religion, in our home. Such things were never spoken of, except as object lessons in the folly of trusting one's life to fables, myths, and superstitions. Reason was our God, Mathematics was his Son, and Science was his Holy Ghost."

The music ceased, then started up anew. *Forlorn Hope Fancy* filled the air within the church, persistent as the light that emanated from the presence of the spirit messenger. She played alone, and suffered him to speak.

"With mighty trepidation, and an inward sense of shame, I took the book into my room, and hid it in the case of my guitar, where I knew no one would ever look. Guiltily I read it, thinking all the while that I was doing something wrong. Temptation, though, proved irresistible.

"I read it three times over. And while it isn't true that I became religious, or even theistic, on account of those first readings, yet it resonated with me. The history . . . the allegory . . . the poetic beauty of it all. Somehow it dovetailed with my love of music, and the wonderful sensations that came over me each time I held my instrument and played. Without knowing it, or perceiving its effects on me, I began to feel a connectedness to things outside of my cognition; beyond, even, the boundaries of mind and thought."

XVI.

HE SAT UPRIGHT in bed, a book in hand. Suddenly the door flew open wide. He quickly threw the book aside and ventured nonchalance, without success. His mother looked upon him from the doorway, quizzically, yet noncommittally.

"What are you doing in here?"

"Nothing," Aaron faltered.

"Nothing?" she replied. "You're doing *something*, if only sitting there staring at the wall. What's that you've got?"

"A book."

"What book?"

He shrugged and offered no response. She neared the bed, and took the book up from the place where it had come to rest. Holding it cautiously in one hand, she lightly thumbed the leaves, and made a show of scanning them, although her eyes were fixed upon her son. The look she cast upon him was foreboding.

"Getting religion, are we?" she inquired, in a voice gone completely flat.

"It's just a book," he said, his face a fiery red.

"Yes, just a book," she said. "You know, Aaron," she continued, her voice softening, "it's not that I completely disapprove. There are things in that book which everybody needs to know; has a *duty* to know, if it comes to that. For better or worse — probably for worse — the sentiments it expresses have made our world what it is today. It has had an incredible, almost hypnotic influence over the minds and emotions of people who ought, really (based on what we know of them) to have known better. Read it, Aaron, but don't be one of them. Let your character mature, untainted by fanciful things. Be adventurous if you must, but always wise."

So saying, she tossed the Bible back toward the bed, as if it were a filthy rag, then shuddered, turned, and left the room without a word, noiselessly closing the door behind her.

He sat there several minutes, motionless. Once again the door moved on its hinges, and his older brother stepped inside.

"Where's this book you've got?" he queried, in a voice that was laughing, scolding and disgusted all at once. He spied the Bible, lying on the bed at Aaron's feet, and took it up.

"Holy . . . Bible," he intoned, deliberately reading out the words upon the spine. "What are you doing with this swill?"

"Just curious," his brother said, laconically.

"Are you *sure* it's only curiosity?"

"Of course I'm sure."

"You're not in here *praying*, are you, behind closed doors?" asked Wolf.

"Don't be ridiculous. Of course not."

"Or sacrificing goats, or any of that voodoo? Because if you are, I . . . ."

"I found the stupid thing, and just started reading it, because I wanted to!" cried the boy, in a burst of indignation. "Ma told you, didn't she?"

"She's crying," said Wolf. "You've got her all upset. She thinks she's failed you."

"I didn't mean to hurt her," said the lad. "It's just a book, and I was only curious, that's all."

"I know, I know," said Wolf, "you told me that." But there was a patronizing air of faux empathy in the way he spoke the words. "Never mind. She'll get over it. But will you?"

Mischievously he grinned.

"Get over what?"

"The seduction of it all. The overpowering, enervating effect it has on everything that makes you human and sets you apart from the lesser species, which is Reason, and the ability to see the world as it really is, and not as some bizarre fantasy where you trade your dignity and self-respect, your life in fact, for the far-off promise of something you will never know, because it can't possibly exist. It's like a drug, you know. Makes you feel good. Mmmmmmmm."

"You needn't fear for me," was Aaron's curt reply.

"I'm not so sure of that," said Wolf. "But I'll keep an eye on you, and if I see the signs . . . ."

"Go away, please, Wolf," he begged.

"Sure; sure. It's dinner-time. Are you coming?"

"I'll be down."

"Good. Ma's alright. She'll be better when you get there." He paused at the door. "Oh, and Aaron . . . ."

"Yes?"

"Don't forget to wash your hands."

He winked, then out he went.

XVII.

SUDDENLY, THE music ceased.

"From that point, I believe that every iota of respect he might have felt toward me was forever gone."

"And yet," observed the ghost, "you never flagged in *your* respect for *him*."

"That is true," said Aaron, thoughtfully.

"In spite of the contempt he showed toward you, and the cruel jibes and taunts with which he never failed to mock you?"

"Yes, despite all that."

"Nothing more?"

"If I understood it I would tell you," he declared.

"Then I will tell *you*," she said. "Your faith and loyalty were as much a symbol of the good in you as his loathing and contempt were of the evil force that dwelt in him."

The spirit turned away from him, and on her lute began to play a piece to which her whole attention now was drawn. Enchanted, Aaron watched. The melody was quick and bright, yet strangely melancholy in its over-all effect, like Hope imbued with elements of Doubt, or Happiness alloyed with a shadow of Regret. Her style of play was perfect — neither diffident nor ostentatious. She finished with a rapid tremolo that held both theme and mood directly to the end, exhilarating in its force, though played on such a peaceful instrument.

"Who wrote that piece?" he asked.

"John Dowland," she replied. "*The Tremolo Fantasy*, or so it's styled. Sometimes misattributed, but Dowland through and through."

"I think so too," he said. "You know it for a fact?"

"I am with him now, as he composes it."

Another pause ensued. It was a lengthy one.

"I do not like to think," spoke Aaron finally, "that Wolf was evil."

"No man *is* evil," she asserted. "But evil finds a haven

in his thoughts. It bides there silently until resistance ebbs, then makes its way into the world, as wicked words and deeds."

"He spoke of good, and seemed committed to it. Even before I was old enough to fully understand, I could see that he possessed a deep empathy for the human race, and that he aspired to use his gifts on its behalf. He would end injustice; find a cure for cancer; develop some wonderful means to feed the poor. But . . . it really makes no sense, and I hardly know how to say it. But at some point it seemed that all his aspirations merged into a single, indefinable sort of idealism, completely at odds with the objective rationality that he professed."

"Sincere?" the ghost inquired.

"Oh yes!" he gushed. "Sincere! A sincerity borne out by the total self-denial with which he followed his ideals. His health; his appearance; even his means of sustenance, he set aside, as first one vision was pursued and then the next. And then at some point, only vaguely definable, I could see that all his aspirations seemed to meld into that one single, unifying belief, the nature of which I could never fully understand. Somehow, at its core, I think it had to do with a sort of fatal shortcoming involving human progress . . . that Mankind had gotten itself on the wrong track, and that by correcting itself in that regard might atone for all its faults and come at last unto a state of peace, and justice, and plenitude for all. Something that he longed for with all his heart, but that he knew, in his heart of hearts, would never come to pass. How could it, when it contradicted human nature, which no ideal or ideology could change? The gist of it, I think, was that he saw injustice in the world, and couldn't square it with the lofty notions he embraced. And then . . . ."

"He changed," the ghost rejoined.

"Yes," said Aaron, darkly. "A change came over him . . . a change in how he viewed the world. His former faith became a loathing of the human race, and even more, a loathing of himself. His character grew ugly, dark and grim. He lashed out at the world, and turned to violence, of a petty and vindictive kind. I challenged him. You know it all. At last he cast off everything, and severed ties with all humanity. He lived his life out penniless and sick. But in so doing, he renounced violence. I was glad of that."

"He *told* you he renounced it," said the ghost.

"If he told me, it was true. Wolf always kept his word. Above all else, he was an honest man . . . ."

Darkness suddenly prevailed, as all the ghost's unearthly light went out, leaving Aaron sightless in a gloom that wrapped itself around him like a shroud.

"Margaret?" spoke Aaron, in a voice of alarm. "Margaret? Are you there?"

"I am here," her voice sounded, near at hand, but with a different timbre, fainter than before.

"What has happened to the light?"

To this came no reply.

"Have I died?" he mused aloud, "or has my vision failed? Where is my lute? Margaret? Let me see you once again!" The words were spoken with subdued anxiety: soft and even, yet with urgency.

"I am here," he heard her say again, from somewhere near at hand. And even as she spoke, her light began to manifest itself within the limits of the space in which he stood.

XVIII.

VANISHED WAS THE inside of the Old Grace Church. As light and vision both returned the inner trappings of his little house appeared. The spirit stood before him in her light, attired not as she had been before, but in a long and hooded robe of coarse black cloth. The robe was gathered at her waist and terminated just above her naked feet.

"What has happened?" Aaron asked.

With ghostly mien the spirit and her light progressed toward him.

"This is a poor, and miserable place," she spoke in reverie. "Small, and cold, and damp, and drab. You have hardly room to move about. There is little comfort for the body, and nothing here to soothe and cheer the mind. Not a sprig of holly to remind you of the season, and the meaning it portends. You pride yourself in this, I think?" she asked, emerging from her pensive state.

He started to reply, then failed.

"Have you been happy here?" she asked.

"I have been content," was his reply. He hung his head, as if ashamed.

"Content to languish in unhappiness," she sighed. "I'll say no more of that. It wasn't to accuse."

"No; no," said Aaron, as he turned his gaze from her. "Reproach me for it if you must. I won't resent it. There's been a change in me, and I can hardly tell you what it is. Must we stay here?"

"No," the ghost replied. "But tell me why you ask?"

"I think . . . . I think . . . ." He faltered with uncertainty, but as he spoke the words came with conviction. "I don't like this place. I don't want to dwell here any more. For some strange cause it fills me with an inner chill; an inward sense of darkness and despair I never felt before."

"When did this change transpire?"

"When first I saw you in the church," he said, "and saw

the light you carry, beating back the darkness, which could not stand up to it. When was it? It seems so long ago. Must we stay here? Is there no place else where I can go?"

"This is your point of origin," she declared. "This is where you begin. Go forth from here and walk."

"Walk where?" was his inquiry.

"Walk where you will," she answered him.

"Alone?" he asked.

"Alone, but not alone," she spoke. "There is the door, behind you. Go now, Aaron. Go."

The light began to fade, and with it every aspect of the ghostly being. By her light's last glimmering he stepped toward the door, but as he did, it slowly opened of its own accord, manipulated by an unseen hand. Complaisantly, and with a gentle tread, he stepped into the night.

Into a different world he stepped. Not different preternaturally, as might have been supposed (given what the ghost had shown him heretofore), but in a manner closer to reality, odd and disconcerting though it was. Clear was the sky; the air both dry and mild. No hint of snow appeared, nor any sign that snow had fallen recently. A bright full moon hung overhead, irradiating all within his ken, and showing Aaron that some change had taken place since he had left his house that night.

For just a trice he stood bemused, to see his little dwelling in the form in which he first set eyes on it, an unused shed, not fit for habitation. The leafless branches of an ancient maple tree grew up against its eaves unpruned — a tree cut down by Aaron's hands some thirteen years ago. He looked about to see things extant that no longer were, and things not present that he knew would come to be.

"Strange," he mused aloud. "Let's see where this will lead." And so, as Margaret bade, he walked, his destination undisclosed, beyond the graveyard, past the Old Grace Church (whose aspect bore an oddly younger look), beyond the pastor's house (where all the lights were out) and straight into the street. There he turned and made his way, along the limits of the church's grounds. Reaching the terminus of this boundary, he turned once more and crossed the road into a narrower and darker thoroughfare, whose street lights shone but dimly with a yellow glow, not brighter than the moon above. Houses lined this thoroughfare, though scarcely visible, set back some distance from the street, and partially obscured by tall fir trees, some of them adorned with Christmas lights of white and blue. His footsteps sounded with their muted tread upon the pavement as he walked, with measured cadence and a speed not lessened by the notion that he knew not where he went. No other sound regaled his ears. But for the noise of his feet, he might have been struck deaf for all he knew.

He turned into a second street, much starker in its aspect than the last, where simple houses glistened in the lamplight. Though small and modest in appearance, many were adorned with symbols of the season. He walked past scenes of the Nativity, which clashed with worldly symbols of the time. Plastic Magi bearing plastic gifts kneeled solemnly in front of plastic mangers, where they vied with plastic snowmen, plastic Christmas trees, and teams of plastic reindeer, drawing plastic sleighs with plastic Santas lugging sacks of plastic toys. Not a light shone in the windows of these houses, yet from the quiet aspect of the still and solemn atmosphere, one might have thought that every human inmate whom they sheltered now lay resting in the soft and kind narcotic of forgetful sleep.

All but one, perhaps. For now, capriciously, he stopped before a house of faded brick, no different than the rest, yet bare of decoration. He stopped before this house, then stood in contemplation for a minute's time.

"Wolf's house," he spoke aloud.

Suddenly a door hinge squealed, and from its door a human form emerged. Clad in white from head to toe, his features hidden by a broad-brimmed hat, this person walked in lengthy strides toward the very spot where Aaron stood. So briskly and intent upon his progress did he go, that Aaron was obliged to step away, lest both collide. And in that instant when he stepped aside, the interloper raised his head, disclosing as he did the black man's face.

His visage wore a look of deep disdain. Not an evil look as such, but one replete with meaning, if it might have been deciphered. The black man's eyes met Aaron's own, and quickly fell. And then he promptly hastened off, with no time left for speech between the two. He merged into the darkness of the street, intent upon his goal, whatever goal it might have been.

Resolved upon a purpose of his own, Aaron turned toward his brother's house, walked quickly to the door, and resolutely rang the bell.

The door squealed once again, a light shone in his eyes, and presently he was looking at his brother's face. Not in the manner he had seen it last, as just a shadow lurking out of sight, but through the very eyes of what had been his younger self, facing Wolf as he had faced him years ago, within that very time and space.

"It took you long enough," he said, as Aaron walked inside. His words reverberated from the walls. The house was bare, so far as could be seen, completely nude of all effects, including furniture. Only a bag — a sturdy-looking canvas bag — reposed upon the floor. A single light bulb on the ceiling feebly lit the hallway where the two men stood.

"I read your letter," Aaron said. "I worked all night, and

found it in the mail when I got home. I came as quickly as I could."

"I need your help," spoke Wolf. "You see that bag?"

"Yes, I see it."

"It has to go somewhere."

"I can take it," Aaron said.

"Not just anywhere. Here's an address."

Wolf handed him an index card.

"That's just a street address. Is there a name?"

"No, there's not a name."

"Whom do I give it to?"

"You don't give it to anyone. Just take it as near to that place as you can, and don't if you can help it let yourself be seen."

Aaron eyed his brother with suspicion.

"What's in it?" he inquired. He knelt down to examine it, but drew back on the sudden when the object moved, and from within a muted noise came.

"Is that a cat?" he asked, bemused.

"No, it's a bag," his brother sneered.

"It *is* a cat," cried Aaron, wonderstruck. "Why have you put it in a bag? Can it even breathe?"

"Of course it can breathe, stupid," Wolf replied. "Do you think I'd have put it in there if it couldn't? The fact is that I've used that cat to do research, and now I've finished with him. He can go back to the place where he was found."

"What research?" inquired Aaron.

"Don't ask," was Wolf's retort. "You wouldn't understand."

"I might, if you explained it patiently."

"There's no point in it. All the patience in the universe couldn't breach the walls of your stupidity. Suppose I told you," he went on, tantalizingly, "that I'd discovered a cure for one of the oldest and most virulent diseases known to man? Would that impress you?"

"How could it not?" said Aaron.

"Well, I haven't. But it's not for want of trying. Suppose I told you I was close?"

"Why, that would be fantastic!" Aaron cried.

"Yeah it would. So now I need your help, and even though it's just a little thing, don't go asking all kinds of questions and trying to put me on the spot. Take it for what it is. You'll have a hand in something big . . . something bigger than both of us. Something to make them stand up and take notice."

"I'm sure," said Aaron, thoughtfully, "that I've no interest in *that*."

"Maybe not," his brother said. "But I do. And if you were smart, which you're not, you *would* take an interest in it. Perhaps it might goad you into making something of yourself. But that's not my concern. It ought to be, since you're my brother, but I've got other things to think about right now. I see you're looking all around and trying to figure out why everything's so cold and bare. Well, I've sold the joint. Next week we close, and this will be my last night here."

"You've sold your house? But why?"

"Simply put, I need the money," Wolf replied. "It's all tied up right here. With help from outside sources I can live on it for years." He looked at Aaron meaningfully.

"You have to live somewhere," protested Aaron.

"Oh, don't strain your noodle over that. Come spring and I'll be moving to the hills, to a pleasant little piece of land I've bought. Rough living, but it suits my needs."

"What about your work?"

"I'll finish what I'm doing now and then I'll call it quits. Call it an early retirement."

"But that's absurd! You're thirty-three years old! Who retires at that age?"

"Who *wouldn't*, if he could? That is to say, if he had the common sense and fortitude to leave the never-ending rat race of modern life and all of its attendant miseries? *You* should try it. Maybe it would help to cure those ideas you've got about magical non-entities in the sky."

He sighed and shook his head. "But I suppose that's never going to change. Just do me that favor, will you, with the pussy-cat?"

"Sure, Wolf," Aaron said, submissively.

"You see that length of string, tied to the zipper tab? When you get to where you need to go, put the bag on the ground, stand back three feet, and use that string to open it. Don't worry about the cat, he'll pop right out of there. And don't get anywhere near him, because he's madder and meaner than hell. Once he's made his getaway, you get yourself away, as quickly as you can, without making yourself conspicuous. Never mind the bag, just leave it there and don't go near it. Don't touch it, do you hear? Do it all tonight, while it's still dark. From here, directly. Don't go anywhere else until it's done."

"Is that all?"

"For now, yes. I'll let you know if — and when — there's something else."

"Don't you need a place to stay?"

"No, I've arranged for that. I'll take twenty or thirty dollars, if you've got it."

He fumbled in his pocket and produced some folded notes. He counted out the cash and handed it to Wolf, who took it silently, without a word of thanks, as if it were his own.

"Go on, get out of here," said Wolf. He pointed to the door, a gesture of impatience. Picking up the bag he handed it to Aaron. "Go!"

Aaron took the bag in hand and left. Exiting the house, he turned and gave his brother a beseeching glance. The countenance of Wolf was cold and stern. The porch door closed, and once again he found himself alone, amidst the moonlit darkness of a quiet street.

XIX.

AND SO HE carried on, through those deserted streets, until at last he found himself within an alleyway, behind the place whose address Wolf had scribbled on the card. A street lamp thirty yards away gave light enough by which to see. A close-grown row of Arborvitae trees set off the alley from the yard which it abutted. Aaron stopped, and set the bag down on the alleyway. Then he paused and looked about, first right, then left, then to his rear. He undertook those actions twice.

Without a pause he knelt down carefully and grasped the coil of twine connected to the zipper's end. Obeying his instructions, Aaron stood back from the bag as far as practical, and gently pulled. The zipper gave way readily. There came at once a frantic stirring of the feline trapped inside, as if the creature knew that freedom was at hand. Like an infant being birthed, its head appeared within the cleft, then straightaway its upper arms emerged, soon followed by a wriggling trunk, and finally a pair of thrashing legs.

And so the deed was done. The animal, now set at large, looked dazedly about, then bounded off with lightning speed behind the Arborvitae and was gone.

A curious transformation now occurred, and Aaron found himself an entity detached. The man that he had been so long ago walked quickly from the place where he had stood, and vanished in the heavy shades of night. Aaron mused upon the oddity of having been that man, speaking words that he had spoken on that night and seeing things that he had seen, as if the past and present had conjoined.

Down the alleyway he gazed. The craggy limbs of leafless trees, which grew on either of its sides, appeared to meet and form a tunnel, like a passageway. He hesitated now, uncertain what to do, or where to go. Suddenly, as if on instinct, Aaron stepped toward the passageway.

"Not a word of protestation," said a voice to his rear. "Not a single question as to what, wherefore, and for the benefit of whom."

He turned to see the black man, looking at him with a contemplative eye.

"Explain?" he asked, defiantly.

"You require it? But why?"

"Because you're being cryptic," Aaron said. Both men's words were spoken just above a whisper, low in register. "I'm not at all sure what you mean."

The black man gave a sneer, and looked askance.

"Your brother tasked you with a chore."

"He did."

"He asked for money."

"Yes he did."

"You gave it to him."

"Yes I did."

"Why?" A pointed question, quickly, bluntly, and directly asked.

"He was my brother, sir," was Aaron's curt reply.

"And never did you think," the black man carried on, as if the words had never reached his ears, "to make the least inquiry as to what he was about. Or . . . ."

"He was my *brother*, sir," said Aaron, interrupting.

"Oh, indeed!" the black man cried. "That explains it, I suppose!"

"Explains what?" demanded Aaron.

"Your willful ignorance, I'd say . . . your utter lack of curiosity. What is this animal, this cat? What a strange request, that you should bring it to this place, and leave it here. Why here, of all places? Why the mystery; the secrecy?

Oh, he was your *brother* ! What wouldn't you do for your *brother*, whose best idea of brotherly affection consisted of his spitting on you every chance he got? Oh, for such a *brother*! But tell, me, truly, *why*? Why blind yourself to all reality?"

"It wasn't for the likes of me to question him. He was a man of science, a brilliant man. I didn't share his knowledge, or his intellect, and couldn't parley with him. He had his motives and his reasons, none of which I understood. He was my brother and he needed help. That's all I knew."

"All?" the black man asked.

"I don't know what you mean." Aaron's hands were clenched; his eyes averted.

"I mean," the black man said with guile, "that possibly your darling Wolf was much more than you built him up to be, within your wildest dreams. Stay! No more. I'll leave it up to you, my friend. I asked you yesterday to visit me, and will you do it now? I think you will this time!"

"I think not," Aaron answered, forcefully.

"Oh, I think *so*!"

"I don't know where you live."

"You lie. Don't you recall? You told me once before. You said — implied it, rather — that I lived in Hell."

"So I did," was the retort. "And so you do. But I'll not visit you."

149

"Tsk, tsk," the black man clucked. "Such spite! Perhaps," he spoke, in tones of confidence, "were you to know just where your interests lay, you wouldn't take that tack. What of that?" he shrugged. "You're free to please yourself, in all regards. Look down that path, however, past the light, to where the prospect narrows and the lines converge. Hell, my home, lies there, beyond that place."

He held his arm aloft and stretched it out, toward the passageway. The motion was a sweeping arc.

"Deep, impenetrable Hell. Known by all, but seen by few, and understood by none. That cryptic place where Truth shines bright, and knowledge of the self sets ignorance at naught. A place of revelation. I offer not a picture, but a view. Aaron, will you come?"

"I will not come."

"You will find a gracious host . . . ."

"I will not come."

"Astounding things, no man has seen before . . . ."

"I will not come."

"Knowledge, in its purest form . . . ."

"I *will not come*. Why do you persist? I will not come for all your blandishments. Now go away! I have a purpose here, and you're impeding it!"

The black man smiled.

"I'll wait for you," he said, his eyes afire. "For you the

way is free. Come to me when your purpose is fulfilled. Come when the fleeting time best suits your needs."

His eyes afire with an impish light, the black man ambled with a doughty tread toward the passageway. He whistled as he went. Aaron followed with his eyes until the black man passed the point where the perfect blackness met imperfect light, and there he vanished out of view.

Aaron stood alone and still, reflecting on the words that he had heard. Presently he turned about, as if to leave the place. Something made him pause. And suddenly he turned once more, to face the passageway.

"I will come," he said. And down the passageway he went.

XX.

A FEARFUL DARKNESS fell upon him, of a blackness so intense that it could not be seen, and a silence so profound that it could not be heard. Directionless he walked within the void, guided by he knew not what. Heedless of a stumble; mindless of those obstacles that might have blocked his way, he journeyed at a walker's pace, intent and confident.

Miles and miles he carried on, within a span of time that seemed to him like days, or months, or even years. Still he walked unwearied. A voice rose up from the lightless gloom, and spoke to him in words that sounded strangely like his own. Yet they were not his words, nor echoes of his thoughts, but fell upon his mind unsought, from somewhere in the unseen space in which he walked entombed.

"Your willful ignorance," the voice said. "Your utter lack of curiosity."

His voice, not his words. It came from this side, then from that; now from behind, and now before. *His* voice, as if he stood beside himself, discoursing with himself, in whispered words that formed an argument, whose meaning he could not divine.

"The cat," the voice said. "What did it mean? Wolf. The money. Why? Had he no money of his own? What did he spend it on? How much did you give him, in the course of all those years? Thousands. What did he spend it on? You never asked. A scientist, a brilliant man. An honorable man, renouncing violence. The cat. The snow. Christmas. It was Christmas of that year. The year before you cast off everything and settled at the Old Grace Church. Do you remember now, how good it felt to be away from worldly cares, and liberated from the chains of thought? Work! That peace of mind which physical exhaustion brings! And then the dream *would* come! The cat! The snow! Your willful ignorance! The fear that thought would drive you to . . . the knowledge . . . of . . . ."

"Of what I dared not think," he said aloud.

"Of what you dared not think," the voice whispered, echoing his words. "And yet the dream would come. But you denied it every time, and stopped your ears before the truth might out. Don't you see the light ahead? What is that light ahead?"

"A pinprick," Aaron said aloud, "of something not as black as that which walls me in. A pinprick, hardly worthy of the name."

For he had seen the speck of light, and now upon that light he fixed his eyes. With faintest magnitude it shone, illuminating nothing. And yet by contrast with the heavy cloak of blackness that enrobed his being and purloined his sight, the point of light shone as a thing conspicuous; a thing of wonderment.

The voice ceased, and nothing in the void dwelt save Aaron Westwode and that speck of light. Onward he continued, never faltering, but set upon his purpose, while the speck remained a speck, unchanged. Onward he pursued, until at last, as if it acted on its own caprice, the point of light enlarged. Its growth was small, yet unmistakable, and as he walked the point grew with every step.

Presently, a strange and eerie light appeared, along the borders of his path, revealing to his sight the prospect of an orchard, vast and overgrown. It glowed but dimly, like the gloaming, though by it he could see the knotted trunks and unkempt branches of the trees, all nude of leaf, and growing wildly on a soil strewn with rotting leaves and fallen boughs.

And though the light glowed on the edges of the path he trod, the blackness of the sky did not abate. Now from the ground a smoking mist arose, and wafted slowly up in wisps of ghostly steam, that clung to every tree and made it black and wet. The prospect never changed as Aaron moved along, for it was vast, and stretched eternally on either side.

Diverted for the moment by the changes he perceived, he presently revived, to focus his attention on the distant light. He looked now to behold that in the interval its magnitude and brightness had again increased. Now it waxed, with each and every step he took, until at last its provenance was clear. The object was a window, fixed to some odd structure unrevealed.

A solitary window, gushing light. Aaron stopped, and stood in contemplation of the thing he saw. Silence now gave way to sound, as from the object, distant fifty yards from where he stood, the din of music could be heard. It struck his senses as a feeble tickling, pleasant to perceive, though indiscernible as anything but music, faint and insubstantial in its form.

But as he drew still closer to the light, the sound resolved into a rhythmic tattoo of staccato notes, alive and
gay, and of a timbre like a harpsichord. Closer still he drew
toward the sound, and knew, at last, the music so adeptly
being played.

"*The King's Hunt*," Aaron mused, aloud.

And so it was. But now it could be clearly seen that
light and sound flowed from the window of an edifice both
queer and void of logic in the context of the place wherein
he stood. This structure was a hut, in aspect like the dwelling of some Zulu shaman, sided all about in grass, and
roofed in tightly-layered thatch. Its shape was of a mush-
room, twelve feet in diameter and rising from the ground,
with walls eight feet in height, and topped off with a low,
domed roof. A single window, rudely-cut and open to the
air, adorned it on the side that Aaron faced. The light had
shone therefrom.

For just a moment Aaron paused, and stared in wonder at this curiosity. The music ceased, and all was sound-
less once again. Cautiously, with trepidation in his step, he
neared the little shack, and coming to the window, peeked
inside.

He peeked inside to see the black man, seated on
a wooden bench before an antique virginal. Directly he
began to play, and from the outset Aaron knew the piece

as John Bull's famous work, *In Nomine IX.* With verve and energy he played, exceeding his performance at the Old Grace Church. He wore a garish costume, clubbed together from a long doublet, knee breeches, white hose, waistcoat, frilly cuffs, and buckled shoes, all topped off with a wide cravat, whose ends flowed downward in a lacy pattern, covering his breast.

With gaudy showmanship he smote the instrument. The black man played with tempo quick, and energetic touch upon the keys. To and fro his body swayed, in movements both pronounced and sharp; not uncontrolled, but fraught, it seemed, with some allusive meaning, vital to the work. At intervals he closed his eyes and smiled, as if in pleasure's throes. And though he had the window to his back, at one such interval it seemed he turned his head and smiled, as if he knew that Aaron stood there, watching him in awe.

Virtuosi by the thousands might have played that complex piece, and yet no human talent could have played it as the black man did. There was magic in his touch, at once commingling all the features of an art that had within its scope the power to enchant, bewitch, and woo. So deftly did he play that Aaron might have sworn that he could hear the music, see the music, feel and smell, and taste the music too. Enchanted was the virginal itself, enduring an abusive style of play that would have razed its mortal counterpart.

With untamed strength the black man played the piece. Having reached the summit of its heights, he brought it hurtling downward to the nadir of its end. Coming to the final chord, he hovered on its brink for one dramatic instant. Down, then, came his fingers, hard upon the keys, and held that chord with force, as if to make the sound remain, suspended in the air, for all time yet to come. And in that denouement, the black man closed his eyes, drew his breath in deep, then loosed it with a long, contented sigh. It faded, like the notes, into a realm of naught.

XXI.

THEN UP HE sprang again, his green eyes all ablaze, as on his heels he twirled about and faced his visitor.

"Aha!" he cried, with unalloyed glee. "You have come! I knew you would! Did I not tell you so? And here you are! Welcome, Aaron Westwode! Welcome!"

He held his arms out wide, and smiled so broadly that the corners of his mouth seemed like to split.

"Welcome to my home!" he bellowed, dancing as he did a sprightly jig. "Don't stand there gaping, like a fool! Aaron Westwode is no fool! Enter! Enter! Enter!"

Invitingly, impatiently, he beckoned. "The door, my friend! The door! There, beside you, to your left!"

Aaron looked askance to see a door, where at the outset no door had been seen. It was a simple door — a pile of rotting sticks, that sagged upon the hinges holding it, and seemed to offer nothing but an ingress, or an egress, since a barrier to passage it was not. Its fastening was an ancient rusty latch. The door was close at hand, yet Aaron balked.

"Enter! Enter! Lift the latch and come inside!"

His hand was on the latch, and still he balked.

"Have you come this far for nothing?" The black man thrust his head completely out of window. "Lift! Lift! Lift it up, my faithful friend, and enter my abode!"

Lifting up the latch, he pulled the door toward him and was greeted by an avalanche of light that made him wince as if in pain. Notwithstanding this, he boldly crossed the threshold and directly stepped into the tiny hut.

The tiny hut? Wonderful to say, Aaron looked about to find himself, not in the little hut, but in the vast and empty nave of a cathedral.

A cathedral, in the Gothic style. The black man stood before him, clothed in strange raiment, and laughed until the echoes of his laughter sounded all across the limits of the hollow nave.

"Welcome!" he exclaimed, as tears rolled down his face.

His fit now at an end, he grinned again from ear to ear, and once more danced his lively jig.

"What place is this?" asked Aaron, looking dazedly about. Indeed, the contrast overwhelmed his sense, and forced him to accept in little time a change that he had not foreseen in any way, however small.

Dwarfed to insignificance, both figures stood engulfed within a sea of stone and space. Flanking the nave on either side, a high arcade of clustered columns, dainty in appearance, radiated up and outward to support a vaulted roof, so lofty in its elevation as to make vertiginous any who surveyed its heights. In the clerestory above, rows of pointed arches framed an ocean of stained glass, depicting scenes obscured by distance from the floor below.

"This is Hell," the black man said. "Behold!"

Deferring to his host's desire, Aaron scanned the prospect all about. Behind him stood the narthex, with its triple portals closed; at his sides the high arcades, with parallel aisles both left and right; to the front the quire, beyond which nothing could be seen. Many wondrous things regaled his eyes, each a marvel in its own, and beggaring description as a whole. Most curious of all, the light by which the edifice and all its objects showed, sprang not from sunlight, streaming into apertures contrived by human craft, but from a spectral glow, far different from all the ghostly lighting Aaron yet had seen. It shone like incandescence from the atmosphere above, and cast hard shadows from the objects that it struck.

"Hell as a cathedral?" Aaron spoke at last. "What sort of hell is that?"

"A proper hell," was the reply. "Not a hell of pain and misery; of never-ending torture, as you foolish beings like to think, but one of honesty and truth, wherein my light shines over all."

"What is truth to you?"

"Truth," he said, "is antidote to lies. How the world maligns me, as it taints me with each slander that its malice can devise!" He smote his breast. "How it *pains* me! "How it *rends* my heart!"

He shrugged.

"Yet I endure. Behold this beautiful creation. What is a cathedral but a place of light? And what is light, if not a metaphor for truth? The builders of cathedrals sought the light, recruiting every trick of human craft to make it manifest in what they wrought."

"They rather sought," said Aaron, "to recruit the human mind, and bring it nearer the celestial."

"Oh yes, that too," the black man answered, waving his hand dismissively. "Of course you understand," he slyly said, with qualifying nuance in his tone, "for all their cleverness, they failed in that."

"How so?"

"You need to ask? Isn't it obvious? They never dreamt that their celestial goals might have the opposite effect . . . to overwhelm the senses of the worshipper, and make him feel but small and worthless in the eyes of both himself and the Creator. A miserable atomy in the grand scheme of his Maker!"

His last words echoed loudly in the hollow nave.

"I can't believe it so," said Aaron, following a pause in which he cast his eyes toward the marble floor. "Or, if it's true, that it was what they had in mind."

"Certainly not!" exclaimed his host. "What was it we were speaking of, just . . . was it yesterday? The road to Hell, and noble ends? Otherwise known as best intentions? Ah, well, they did the best they could. But you see, I'm cunning . . . perhaps not so cunning as those genius men, but, well, cunning enough! I took their grand idea and marked it as my own. It all comes back to Truth. To see things as they are, objectively; not colored by equivocation or the vice of self-deceit. We don't make pretexts here, or ravel meaning into twisted knots. In Hell we have but one constraint, which is the truth: *the thing that is.*"

The black man grinned with great self pride, at which his green eyes positively shone.

"Who is this 'we,' of whom you speak? Are they cadres of sub-devils whose assistance you employ? Or are they , as I half-suspect, the legions of the damned, condemned to torture without end?"

"Sub-devils?" cried the black man. "Here? Ha! Ha-ha-ha! Oh, Aaron, you amuse me! I hire no devils, sub or otherwise. What must be done here, I must do myself. As for the damned . . . ."

"Don't try to tell me that you torture them yourself," said Aaron, wryly.

"Torture them? *Torture* them?" Again he laughed aloud. "Mean to tell you that I *torture* them? Ha-ha! A-ha-ha-ha-ha-ha! Aaron, oh Aaron, you're in the rarest form today! But I forgive you."

"Forgive me what?"

"That hoary lie, devised to bring me into disrepute. No better than the blood libel, to blacken my name and make the rabble think the worse of me. I tell you, I am not that way! If people only knew it, they would seek me out, and never shun me, as they do!"

"Pardon me," said Aaron, "if I don't believe you."

"Why should I lie?" the black man pled. "The more so since it's quite against my wont? Listen! The damned are better off in Hell than any other place. Here they feel no torment; feel no pain. Here is only peace and contemplation, free of conflict; free of strife. No soul is carried here, but each comes hither of its own free will. No soul is fettered or constrained to stay; its right is sacrosanct, to leave this place at any time, for any cause. Come, and I will show you!"

He ceased to speak, then turned toward the eastern end of the cathedral, where stood the quire that could not be seen. Away he stepped, toward that murky place, and Aaron followed close behind.

Eerily illumined was the long and hollow nave, and yet, as Aaron strode along, a strange effect appeared before his eyes. Where from a distance nothing past the quire could be seen, it now appeared, the nearer he approached, that nothing stood within that space except a pall of utter black, depending from the arches overhead. Curtain-like, it shut off all beyond from view. Blacker than all black was this partition; so black that it reflected nothing of the dazzling light that glowed throughout the nave, but seemed, by some unfathomable property, to swallow up each ray that fell upon it.

And as they passed from nave to crossing, Aaron looked within the transept wings to see the selfsame cloak of black, conforming to the lines of pier and arch, and cutting off each wing from view within the place where now he and the black man stood.

"What lies beyond that veil?" demanded Aaron, as he looked to one wing, then the other, and turned his sight again toward the quire.

"Night lies there; impenetrable night," was the reply. "Night which you have witnessed as you journeyed here."

Aaron moved toward the quire and thrust his hand within the pall. It disappeared, as if consumed. And when he drew it back, it reappeared.

"There too?" demanded Aaron, pointing to the northern transept wing. "And there?" He pointed to the south.

The black man smiled and shook his head.

"It masks," he said, "a different reality."

"What reality?"

"Shall I show you?"

"By all means, if you will."

With that, the black man stepped into the center of the crossing, turned, and faced the nave. Then, stretching out his arms toward the transept wings, he stood erect, and in a thunderous voice roared out,

"FIAT LUX!"

His words resounded through the halls of Hell. Light began to pour into the transept wings, like water rushing in to fill a void. In fluid waves it moved on either side, inundating darkness in a slow and rolling flood, until the transept was illumined with a brilliance equal to the light that shone within the nave.

XXII.

AND NOW THE black man roared again, with laughter and delight. "Look!" he cried. "Look there! And there!" Not changing his position, he gestured with a movement of each hand toward a transept wing. The light revealed a scene perplexingly surreal. For each end of the transept, north and south, appeared to stretch beyond the limits of the eye, its high stone structures reproduced in perpetuity, until they vanished from his sight, at some place near infinity. Its singular effect was as a pair of facing mirrors, one handing its reflection to the other; the other sending its reflection back; so on and on — a never-ending volley of illusion.

Stranger still, and more distressing to the mind, before each columned pier, a heavy chain depended from a point overhead, and from each chain a hangman's gibbet hung. Chain and gibbet both were formed of shining gold, most beautifully wrought. And in each gibbet stood a human form, arrayed in cerements of purest white.

"Behold!" the black man cried. "In *my* house are many

rooms!" He smiled upon the prospect with an owner's pride.

"Who are these . . . beings?" Aaron asked in wonderment, as now he scanned the endless lines of gilded cages with their shrouded occupants.

"The legions of the damned, of course."

"Then you've lied to me," he said in plaintive tones. "You said the damned were free to come and go; that there were neither fetters nor constraints."

"They are. And there are not," replied his host, speaking now with quiet dignity. "There are no chains; there are no locks. They are not suspended high, as you can see. The damned may step down from their cells at any time they please."

"Cells!" Aaron cried. "I know those things for what they are. They are gibbets . . . heinous instruments of cruel and lingering pain."

"And that is how they were abused," the black man said, "in late benighted times. Not so these! These are habitations of repose and ease. Look at them!" he cried, as leisurely he strolled into the northern wing, with Aaron at his side. "There, and there, and there, and there. Look between those bars, and see the faces of the damned. Calm and placid as the sleeping babe. Observe," he bade. "No locks, no welds. Nothing to stay their owners from egress."

The black man seized the portal of a cage that hung nearby, and swung it open wide.

"Friend!" he called out to that denizen of Hell, whose rest he had disturbed. "Leave your slumbers for a time! Come down and speak with us!"

Upon the speaking of these words, the cage began to move. Slowly it descended, inch by inch, until the base of it had softly touched the floor. That done, the human soul it held turned full about within the limits of its narrow cell and stepped outside.

"Wolf!" cried Aaron, in a tone of disbelief. "What! Are you here?"

His brother stood before him, solemn and serene. Wolf, not hostile and defiant, but peacefully complacent, like a languid thinker, lost in his *pensées*. Nothing did he say, but stared ahead with eyes half closed. His arms hung limply at his sides.

"Wolf!" cried Aaron once again.

At which the dreamer slowly turned his head, with great deliberation in the act. He raised his drooping eyelids, looked upon his brother with indifference, and lowered them again.

"I shall stand here," he proclaimed, "forever."

"Forever, Wolf? How came you here at all?"

"I shall stand here in this place," he muttered, speaking

in a dreary monotone, "for all eternity. And then, when that eternity has passed, I shall stand here once again, for all eternity. And on, and on, until the universe exists no more and then bursts out anew, again, again, and yet again. A cascade of eternities will find me standing here."

"Wolf, please, speak plain to me," his brother pled. "Tell me how and why you're here. Are you distressed? Are you in pain?"

"It was HIM," the damned soul said, and turned its gaze upon the black man standing near at hand. "*He* convinced me, finally, of that for which I used to laugh at you and call you fool . . . that God exists. *He* convinced me that reality was more than Man could measure. *He* was there beside me when I took my mortal life, and only then did he succeed at last, after long, long years of patient work. Dead, I wandered, lost and filled with bitter hatred of myself and all that I had been, until *he* sought me out and led me here, where shame and conscience are subdued, and I found rest in the fraternity of kindred souls. Aaron!" he cried, becoming lively on the sudden. "Brother! I must have a word with you before you've left this place!"

"Have it, then!" the black man loudly shrieked. "Oh, *have* it! Tell him! Tell him all! Tell him *everything*!" he shrieked again, unable to contain himself, or so it seemed. He gestured wildly as he spoke, and hugged himself as if for joy.

"You served me as my useful tool," the spirit said, now looking Aaron fully in the eyes. "Without compulsion, willingly. You gave me money, gratis, and you gave me things in kind. You furnished me the means to practice all the evil that my ugly heart conceived when first I lashed out at the human race. Tell me, brother . . . what did you think I was about?"

"Tell! Oh, *tell*!" the black man cried.

"I don't know," was the reply. "How should I know? It was your affair, Wolf . . . none of my concern." He seemed perplexed, as borne out by his tone.

"Don't try to tell me that you didn't know, or couldn't guess," Wolf said. "The animals . . . the cat . . . the plague. The plague! Now do you understand?"

Silent was the black man now, although his green eyes shone as they had never shone before, and he stood with bated breath, awaiting Aaron's words.

"The plague," said Aaron softly, as he dropped his head. "The plague." The words came from his lips, not as a question, but a simple declaration.

"He knows!" the black man cried triumphantly. "Oh, my heart, he *knows*!"

"As he has always known," the soul of Wolf rejoined. "Always known, but never dared admit. How many were there, brother? Seventeen?"

"Seventeen!" the black man cried with glee.

"Human lives that numbered seventeen," the ghost resumed. "When you released that cat, you let loose plague amongst the people of that town. Seventeen you took with that one act."

"Not least of whom," the black man said, and shook his finger right in Aaron's face, "was that enchanting lute girl and her pretty family! Oh, Aaron! Oh Aaron, dear! To think that it was *you*! His willing dupe! You might have spared them all, but you could never say him nay! 'Give me money, fool!' he says. 'Yes, my brother!' you reply. 'Buy me tickets to the land of plague!' he bids. 'Yes, my brother!' you reply. 'Take this bag and free this cat!' where he knew the pestilence could best be spread. 'No worry!' you reply. 'Am I not my brother's keeper? Give me the address and it is done!' Contemplate it, Aaron, and despair! *Despair*!"

"Wolf," said Aaron, with dejection in his voice that was mirrored in his face, "I trusted you. You gave your word to me, and I relied on it. Will you lay this on me, after all?"

"I lay nothing on you," he replied. "You lay it on yourself. My guilt is mine. Yours is yours to cope with as you will. Look to the Devil there, and let him be your guide. Come, *Satanas*, I have languished in your light too long. Take me back to everlasting night, where lies the peaceful slumber that I crave."

Having said these words, his shade retreated to the gibbet, stood within, and closed the gate behind. At once the gibbet rose, until it stood again upon a level with its peers. The black man walked away. Into the very center of the transept now he strode. Aaron followed, grim of feature, looking like a felon on the gallows' stairs.

Once more, the black man held his hands aloft.

"*In pace requiescat!*" the Devil cried. And with those words a flood of darkness poured into the space that it had occupied before, pushing out the light to which it had succumbed. Aaron and the Devil stood together now, and silence reigned in Hell for an extended span. Aaron sat upon a pedestal, and hid his countenance within his hands.

At last the Devil spoke.

"I'm not without compassion for your plight," he said. Gone was his sardonic tone, supplanted by the voice of concern. It was a soothing voice.

"My plight? What is my plight?"

"You know it, Aaron. As do I."

"Yes, I know it, I confess."

"What do you know? And what do you confess?" They were kindly, empathetic words.

"That I have sinned, and nothing can redeem me."

"In what way sinned?" the Devil asked.

"In that I might have known the evil dwelling in my

brother's mind, yet helped him work that evil on the world. Blind to all he was, when all the while my senses stood intact. Oh, Margaret!" he cried. "Did I as good as murder you, and those you loved? And is it any wonder that you sent me here?"

He wrung his hands, with frightful force.

"Horrible," the Devil said, but still in quiet, comfort-laden tones. "All died wretched deaths, but none more so than lovely Margaret. I think I see her now, alone in that ravine, ablaze with fever; shivering with cold. Struggling to save the ones she loved. Striving vainly, sick from that effect of which you were the cause. You, Aaron . . . you, the cause."

"You needn't say it," Aaron groaned. "I know. God forgive me, how I know!" He groaned again.

"God may forgive you," said the Devil slyly. "But listen to me now. Will you forgive yourself?"

"Forgive myself?" he cried. "How is that possible, when I have been so blind, so willfully and pitifully blind? Never will I cease to bear the torment of this shame! It is mine forever!"

"Yes . . . forever. Do you know the meaning of that word? A heartbeat less than all time is no time. Only as Eternity does time exist. But! Be comforted, my friend!

For here, at hand, I have a healing balm! Look here! Look here, and see what I have made for you!"

Aaron looked above to see a golden gibbet, shining in the otherworldly light. The Devil stood before its open gate. With one dark hand he pointed, and beckoned with the other.

"Be of the damned," the Devil bade. "Fear not the word. Let peace ensue."

Aaron rose, and slowly stepped toward the gilded cage. He held up one pace short.

"No longer," Aaron said, "do you dissemble. This has been your purpose all along."

"My purpose all along," the Devil said, in tones affirmative. "To this end, everything."

"Why?"

"If I tell you why, what difference will it make?"

"None, perhaps," said Aaron, with a sigh. "You have your motives; I my needs. And isn't that enough?"

"It is enough. Now come; proceed." Impatiently he beckoned once again.

"Will there indeed be peace?"

"Yes, yes, peace!" the Devil cried. "The peace you've long pursued but never have attained. The solace that you sought in digging graves, eschewing love, forsaking pleasure and the like, but all in vain!" His agitation now was nearly palpable. "This is what you've wanted all along, and now it's real! Come! Come! Know peace!"

"Peace?" he questioned, musingly.

"Peace!" the Devil cried, and now his tone was one of urgency. "Haste, my friend, you *must* decide, and *now*! The time is now propitious; you must act! Nevermore will this be offered you. A peaceful slumber or eternal pain! Decide! You must decide!"

Aaron paused, then slowly reached toward the gibbet's gate. He touched it softly; almost lovingly. The Devil's eyes gaped wide, as on his lips a smile began to spread.

"But I'm not dead," spoke Aaron, stepping back.

"But are you sure?" the Devil cried, insistently. He clutched the gibbet gate and held it fast. "Sure you didn't die last night, a suicide, a knife plunged through your neck? For all you know your body lies all in a heap upon the floorboards of your pitiful abode, surrounded by a pool of blood, and soon to shock the senses of whoever finds it there! Hurry! Hurry! Little time remains! But one step more! Step up! Ah, *damnation* . . . it's too late, you fool! Too late!"

A tumult sounded at the front end of the nave, and suddenly the doors burst open wide. The light within blew crazily about, as if disordered by some ghostly wind. And there, inside the nave, stood Margaret, surrounded by her light, which superseded all the light of Hell.

XXIII.

BRILLIANT WAS THE light within the Devil's realm, yet all its brilliance shone as but an ember in the perfect aura of the spirit's glow. Effulgent shone her light, displacing all the lesser light before it. She paused a moment in the nave, robed in her single garment all of black, her beauty not unequal to the radiance she bore.

Slowly and with measured tread she moved toward the place where Aaron and the Devil stood transfixed. The Devil's hand still clutched the gibbet gate, his nostrils flaring and his eyes aglow; his thin lips curled up in an angry snarl. As she approached he took his hand directly from the gate and held himself erect, his arms enfolded tight across his chest, and cast a look toward her that was filled with fury and indignant rage.

"What business have you here?" he cried, upon her stopping short. "Begone!" He waved his arms, as if to shoo her from his sight. "Here is no place for the likes of you!" The hatred in his tone was palpable.

"No place for any soul that seeks the truth!" She turned her gaze to Aaron, then back toward the Devil once again. Her voice was low, but carried far and wide.

"How dare you slander me?" he bawled.

"How dare you give me cause?" was her reply.

"This is the dwelling-place where truth resides! Truth, in purest form!"

"Truth alloyed with deceit!"

"There is but one truth — truth itself!" the Devil cried. "Which I, alone, command!"

"But for the presence of your victim, you would never try that cant on me!" exclaimed the ghost of Margaret. "What bludgeons of your truth have you assailed him with?"

"*I* assailed him?"

"You!"

"With truth?"

"With *your* truth," she replied, "Or variations on it you confected for your vile, Satanic work."

"You're simply raving now," he said, dismissively. "My words to him were nothing more than gentle prods, which steered him to a knowledge of himself. Of *that* I told him nothing. He learned it from his brother, who resides with me. Go away you meddler, lest I cast you out of here with force!"

She smiled, a confident and knowing smile.

"You have no power over me," she said, and took a step toward him. As she did, her light collided with his space. He started visibly, and shrank back from the light as if in fear. In doing so, he fell against the golden cage. Its gate swung back with a resounding crash.

"Stop!" cried Aaron, stepping forth. "Let me speak." His passive awe had changed to bold activity, though sorrow and despair still sounded in his voice. "Margaret, he's right. He drove it home to me, but not before the revelation that my brother made."

"Aha!" exclaimed the Devil. "What, pray tell, did he reveal?"

"You know," he sorrowfully replied.

"Ah, yes, but let her in on it! Look at her, she's waiting breathlessly!"

Aaron turned toward the ghost with downcast eyes. "Margaret, I murdered you," he said.

"Murdered me?" she asked, incredulous.

"Your father and your mother too," he carried on. "And fourteen others, all the victims of my crime."

"*Your* crime? Your *crime*?"

"*His crime!*" the Devil cried. "Deny it if you dare!"

"I can't," said Aaron, sorrowfully. "Forgive me please, I beg you Margaret. I gave my brother means to carry out the evil that destroyed you and other innocents. I didn't know . . . didn't *want* to know, though in my heart I must have known full well. For fifteen years I lost myself in mindless work, pushing myself to the point of exhaustion, striving to protect myself from thought, lest thought should lead to contemplation and that in turn to something else too terrible to know. Somewhere deep inside I knew the truth, but never could I free it from my mind. The black man came one day, and from the hour that I first set eyes on him he drew me out. He did it slowly, one insinuation at a time, until at last I suffered him to lead me here . . . ."

"To Hell!" rejoined the Devil. "I'm not ashamed, but *proud*, to say the word! Proud of it, and proud of what I am! Above all proud of this, my native land! Hell, the land of perfect truth!"

"He led me here," continued Aaron, heedless of the rant, "and I came willingly. The truth is out, and though it may be said, and rightly so, that I did not conceive the deed, nor acted out of ill intent, the deed was mine. I can't cast off the memory of what I brought to pass. To think of you as what you were in life, and in that vision see you as you were in death, so horrid to behold . . ." He paused and raised his eyes, as if he might say more, but stopped, and cast them down again.

"And like a true friend, I am here," the Devil chimed. "Not to extirpate the deed itself, for nothing can do that, but to blot out its effects upon the everlasting part of you. Not to cause you to forget, for nothing can do that, but to offer you repose, sweet rest, which no remembrance can disturb. And you must *choose*, no matter who or what the meddling ghost that strives to come between us now. It *shall* be one thing or the other; therefore you must *choose*! Eternal rest, or everlasting shame!"

Aaron looked to Margaret.

"Speak to me," he pled. "I trust your word."

"Tell him what you will," the Devil warned, perceiving she would speak, "but tell no lie! Speak only truth, and I will rest content!" He said it haughtily, as if he knew the rightness of his cause would triumph over all.

"Then you may rest *content*," the ghost replied. "But never satisfied." With that she stirred, and forward stepped until the whole of Aaron's form stood folded in her light. Once more the Devil fell back in alarm. Ignoring him, she fixed her gaze on Aaron, then, with kindly, gentle words she spoke.

"He speaks the truth," she said, "he cannot lie. The guilt and shame you feel are grounded in the truth, although opposed to other truths which this fiend lurking here neglects to tell. Hear me now. Aaron, I have been with you for many mortal years, knowing, even from the outset, that which only now has come to you. I was with you in the graveyard as you labored, day by day, while every year on Christmas Eve I gathered up my spirit-strength to make you see me in an earthly form. It was I who left the lute for you to find, knowing it would bring to you a tiny portion of the happiness and pleasure you denied yourself."

"I wanted to atone," said Aaron, thoughtfully. "For what, I never knew."

"But now you know!" the Devil interposed.

"You know," she spoke to Aaron, "but your inferences are wrong. You never murdered me, or harmed my family. Nor did you murder fourteen others, all the victims of your brother's rage and spite. You had no hand in it, apart from what you did, unknowingly, from love, respect, and brotherly allegiance. You know this, Aaron, dearest one. The Devil won't deny it, for he can't!"

"That's not the point, is it?" was the Devil's hot reply. "Did I ever tell him an untruth?"

"You took a seed, and sowed it deep inside his mind, within a dark and cryptic place, untouched by reason; inaccessible to thought. This, Aaron is his way. You've seen his minions, standing dumb and silent in the dark. Those souls are his, recruited through the very trickery he used on you. He is their collective manifestation. He feeds upon and draws his strength from them. By bringing them together in himself he validates the evil in his heart, and soothes the guilt and shame of crimes for which he never can atone. Peace will come to him at last when every human soul stands hanging in his Hell, degraded and abased as he. Your shame is founded on the love of me, but for the love of me I plead, do not give way! Do not submit to what he calls his Truth, as false and vile as any lies!"

"My truth is pure!" the Devil shrieked. He turned to Aaron in a rage. "I tell you for the last time, Aaron, come to me before the chance is lost! You know the dread alternative!"

"Life, redemption and renewal!" cried the ghost.

"Suffering!" screamed the Devil, with a passion. "Suffering and pain, through all eternity!" He swept his hands majestically, to emphasize the word.

His echoes carried far, and died away within Hell's vast domain. But now, abruptly, Aaron left the safe confines of Margaret's brilliant light and stepped toward the Devil with a movement quick and bold. A smile adorned his face, which showed him resolute. And now, his voice fraught with strength, he spoke.

"You say you cannot lie," he said, at which the Devil struck a wary pose.

"Never," he replied, suspicion showing in his tone. "The power is not mine."

"What Margaret has told me . . . is it true?"

The Devil started visibly. He drew his breath in deeply but said nothing in reply. With hatred unconcealed, he glared at Margaret.

"Is it true?" asked Aaron once again. And once again, the Devil held his tongue.

"I ask you for the final time," said Aaron, "true, or not?" With head held high he stared the Devil down.

"**WITCH** !" the Devil screamed, as on his heel he spun, his arm extended stiffly and his pointing finger fixed on Margaret. His body trembled, and the words that issued from his mouth emerged with spitting force. "You *tramp*!" he cried, "you *filthy* sow! Tell me, *jade*, have you combined with him to humble me; to make a fool of me?"

"Am I to answer that?" asked Margaret. "Answer it yourself! Have we combined to humble you; to make a fool of you?"

"Answer her," said Aaron. "You who cannot lie."

"Confound you all!" the Devil cried out, throwing up his hands. "I'll have no more of this!" Back and forth he strode, across the stony floor. "Get out of here!" he raved. "What need have I of *you*, when there are billions more, imbued with gratitude, not hate? Out! Out, and never let me see you more, for you disgust me, both!"

"And yet no answer?" Margaret pursued.

"I've nothing more to say you!" he said, and turned his back to her. "But *you*," he carried on, addressing Aaron in the direst tones, "remember this! Remember, when your guilt is more than you can bear, beyond your power even to *conceive*, that it was I who offered hope to you, and you refused!"

"Peace, *Diabolos*!" cried Margaret. "Your speech is impotent, your powers of persuasion spent! We'll leave this place, yet first I'll try your honesty once more. What lies beyond that veil of black, where proper churches keep their sacred things? We know what grisly scenes lie *there* and *there*," she said, and looked toward the transept wings. "But what have you secreted *there*?"

She pointed to the quire, draped in black.

"None of your concern!" he shouted out, his voice and demeanor filled with fear.

"Something of concern, I think," she said. Then suddenly she stepped into the crossing, and with bold intent walked straight toward the quire and its veil, the Devil shrinking from her as she went. "Shall we investigate? We shall! What might not *light* reveal?"

"No! No! No!" he pled, and fell collapsing to his knees in front of her. He pressed his hands together in a travesty of prayer. "No light!" he begged. "Not *there*! In Heaven's name, not *there*!"

She looked down on his kneeling form, bestowing as she did a look of pity, mingled with contempt. In an instant it was done. She looked toward the pall, her face directed upward, and her arms extended loosely at her sides.

"*Fiat lux*," she calmly said.

"Noooooo !" the Devil howled.

Bootless was his cry. As Aaron watched, the brighter glow of Margaret's light expanded outward from its source, subsuming, not repelling, all the lesser light in which it was immersed. Now every niche of Hell shone in the purer light, and nothing was concealed.

The echoes of the Devil's cry had scarcely ceased when yet another din arose to take their place. A dismal, droning sound, not less pervasive than the light, crescendoed feebly in the air, before descending to the limit of its depths. Up and down it pulsed, without surcease. A thousand million copies of this wave, each one embellished with its own peculiar tone, contended in a harmony of woe, the dreary lamentation of a billion mourning souls.

The Devil lay collapsed where he had knelt, huddled in a shapeless mass upon the floor. He moaned, he sighed, and wept, with heavy sobs and painful cries, pathetic to be heard. Upon the naked stones he beat his hands, a frightful act of unavailing grief.

Beyond the quire, formerly unseen, within the limits of the sanctuary, dwarfed by mighty structures wrought in stone, a plain and simple altar stood. Upon that spot, miraculously set for all to see, reposed a crèche, depicting Christmas in its primal form — that touching scene that Aaron had beheld in Margaret's home, upon the fatal night so long ago.

"Your father's work?" asked Aaron, tenderly.

"My Father's work," the ghost affirmed. They paused to contemplate the scene. "Let's go," she said at last. "This place is terrible."

Together they proceeded down the nave, toward the triple doors, forbidding in their massive state. Arriving there, they stopped to look again upon the wreck that lay beyond.

"Behold it, Aaron," said his guide. "and learn."

"Will you leave them in that state?" he asked.

"It's but a passing thing," she said indifferently. Yet with these words she gave a sudden nod, at which pure night descended over all. Within the darkness nothing could be seen. And nothing could be heard except the weeping of the Devil, and the moaning of the damned.

XXIV.

WITHIN THE CHURCH he stood alone, in darkness of an otherworldly depth. Within the vestibule he stood, and listened to the soft, enchanting sound that issued from the nave: the voice of a solitary lute. The lute was Margaret's; the voice that of ghostly hands on spectral strings. *O Gloriosa Domina* she played, that pæan to the Virgin Mary, whose notes had issued from the fertile mind of Narvaez, a master of the Spanish lute, who lived and flourished in the sixteenth century.

O Heaven's glorious mistress,
Enthroned above the starry sky,
Thou feedest with thy sacred breast
Thine own Creator, God most high.

Covered in the dense black mantle of the air in which he stood, the ringing notes, with their poignant yet simple harmony, beguiled his mind with an enchantment unalloyed by the sense of sight. He stopped and listened through the first and second *diferencias*, while every other sense held still, and naught remained of his perceptions but the faculty attuned to sound, and the glimmer of an understanding past the realm of thought.

And then, as the last chord of the second *diferencia* rang out, bell-like in its clarity, and echoed in the empty nave, his sense of self returned. Silence followed for a moment, as the third *diferencia* began. Only slightly did he hesitate. Opening the door, he stepped into the space beyond.

He saw her seated in the sanctuary, the lute enfolded in her arms. He saw her as she sat beneath the cross, surrounded by the same soft light that earlier had cloaked the spectres in his home. Transcendent light shone forth, whose glow revealed the forms of objects near at hand, while nothing but a void could be seen beyond. Within that void he saw nothing of himself, nor any portion of the path he softly trod. Pure was the light beyond. Pure was the music that the lady played. The verses he had known, so long forgotten, stirred within his mind.

> *What man had lost in hapless Eve,*
> *Thy sacred womb to man restores,*
> *Thou to the wretched here beneath,*
> *Hast opened Heaven's eternal doors.*

He sat before her now, his own lute resting in his arms. *La Rossignol* they played: *The Nightingale*, a beautiful duet, whose notes recalled the warbling creature's song.

"I have been sick," he said. "Very sick, for a very long time, but now I feel that I am well again, and you have made me so."

Nothing did she say. But she affirmed it in her eyes.

"So many years I've wasted now, in pointless repining. And yet," he mused, "perhaps they've not been wasted after all. For I've been given something that perhaps I wouldn't otherwise have had. I know I can be happy now, although it pains me mightily to think I was the cause, guiltless though I might have been, of so much evil; so much suffering."

"Be reconciled," the spirit said. "It will stay with you forever, a part of what you are. Let it lead you to a sense of justice, which never will you find by striving to atone for other people's sins. Let those who bear the guilt make recompense."

"What of my brother?" Aaron asked. "What will happen to him?"

"Nothing will befall him but the fate he chooses of his own free will, which always will be free, no matter what the state of his existence."

"And will he hang there, gibbeted in Hell, for all eternity?"

The spirit smiled. "Remember, Aaron, that the other world is immaterial. Between it and the workings of the mind there is a nexus, faint but real. Only by means of that connection were you able to perceive a state of things beyond the senses that confine your knowledge to the universe of Time and Form. What you saw was wholly allegorical. You could not have seen it as it truly is."

"Then there are no gibbets?" Aaron asked.

"No gibbets. No Hells within cathedral walls. Nothing of this earth."

"But what will happen to him?"

"Nothing, Aaron. No force will act on him. In many ways, symbolic though it is, a Hell of sorts exists for conscience-ridden souls, who from their knowledge of the guilt they bear cannot aspire to the greater good of God and His Creation. Thus they languish in the other world, unable to accept those higher things Creation has to give."

"Can nothing alter their condition?"

"Suffering and pain," she said. "Freely undertaken, for freedom in this world of ours is absolute. A terrible ordeal, not only in the suffering itself, but in the choice to undergo it for the sake of what it means. But as the ghost of Hamlet's father said, 'this eternal blazon must not be, to ears of flesh and blood.' More I will not say."

"What suffering? What pain?" he anxiously inquired.

"Must you persist?" she asked. "Children barely versed in speech insist on knowing everything! Peace, Aaron; let it be! Already I have shown you much. The knowledge that you seek is far, far, far beyond the limits of the human mind."

"Impossibly complex?" he asked.

"Unfathomably simple," she replied.

"But how, if . . . ." he began.

"Unfathomably simple," the ghost said once again. "Yet even if you understood it, you would not; *could* not, accept it as it is."

"But why?" he asked, persisting.

"It would utterly confound your knowledge of the world . . . the world of Time and Form."

Aaron sat reflecting quietly, in meditation of the deepest kind.

"Unfathomably simple," he repeated dreamily, as if bewitched. Then suddenly he chimed, "But yes, it must be so. How else can one account for the illogic of existence? And speaking of existence, what of God? Of course He must exist!"

"He is everything," she said, and smiled.

"But His nature . . . what of that?"

"Unfathomably simple," she replied.

"Oh!" he cried, in flustered tones. "You exasperate me, Margaret!"

"Not to tease or torment you," she soothed, "but only to prevent you making inferences that lead one from the truth, so far as in one's mind it may prevail. But I may tell you this: God is a spirit, and Man His means of walking on the earth. He shares your joys and sufferings alike. Make His home a pleasant one, and do it not from fear, but love."

"But that," cried Aaron, in astonished tones, "is almost what the Reverend Honeybutter said!"

"A wise man," she declared, with a sweet and heavenly smile. "A wise, wise man, indeed."

"And so he is," said Aaron, as he smiled along with her. "I've got no reason now to put him off, or keep from him my confidence. But tell me, if you can, and if it's not beyond my power to understand: what of Mr. Indigo, that boasting harbinger of perfect truth? Is he truly Satan? What are his powers? Is he the opposite of everything that's good?"

"He is truth without its context," she replied. "Truth clothed in its native garb, bereft of knowledge, wisdom and the force of human reason. His dwelling is within the mind, in caverns inaccessible to thought. That is his earthly guise. His is, within my world, the face of every guilty soul."

"And every guilty mind, in this."

"Tricky and deceitful as the day is long," pursued the ghost, "constrained by truth, as poems are constrained by rhyme and meter."

"God and Satan," Aaron mused. "But where is the dichotomy? Are they not polar opposites?"

At this, the ghost broke out into a laugh, a merry, ringing laugh, so blithe and pretty as to counterfeit in sound the cheery aspect of her bright and lovely face. But Aaron, though he smiled in sympathy, appeared confused, and sought an explanation with his eyes.

"Dear Aaron!" she exclaimed. "That you should ask

me such a thing! But certainly you understand! I'm not a theologian . . . I'm a ghost!" She laughed again, and this time Aaron laughed with her.

But when their merriment was at an end, a silence followed of some little time, concluding when the ghost addressed her lute and played *Farewell*, a melancholy air, both sweet in sound and bitter in the sorrow it evoked. And when its consummation was complete, she gazed at Aaron wistfully and sighed.

"*Farewell*," he said, with sorrow in his voice. "But must it be farewell?"

She nodded in reply.

"Please don't go," he pled.

"My powers won't suffice to keep me here," she said, "though I confess I wouldn't have it so." Quietly she spoke, her voice whisper-soft. "I know that you'll believe me when I tell you it must be."

"I believe your every word," he spoke. "And yet it's hard for me to think of losing you. It fills me full of sorrow, at a time when I perceive that happiness is near. I had thought, perhaps, that you might stay with me and counsel me; make music as we have so beautifully this endless night, and let me joy in your loveliness and light. Margaret! Will I never see you more?"

"Nevermore," she said, with stern finality.

"Margaret, I love you!" Aaron cried. Then suddenly he started up, and with a movement of his arm reached out as if to touch her face. But all her substance faded as his hand approached, dissolving into mist. And only when he drew back did her form return.

"And are you so bemused?" she asked, in softest tones of gentle wonderment. "I see it written on your face. Again I tell you Aaron, I am not a creature of this earth. The action of my essence on your mind has been the cause whereby my figure has been seen; my speech made audible. I am ephemeral, and cannot stay. Listen to me now. Leaving, I return you to the world from which you came. It is your world while you inhabit it — a world where Time and Form pervade the mind, and words alone give shape to thought. Accept that as it is, and always bear in mind that something better, more consistent, lies beyond. Henceforth be happy, since you were meant for happiness, in spite of all those ills that circumstance must bring. Enjoy life, within the strictures of those Godly laws whose purpose is to foster human joy, and not to try the faithfulness of men. That is my valediction, all of it. And know my love is truly yours, as much as ever insubstantial ghost can love a man of flesh and blood."

"And my love yours," was his reply, "as much as man of flesh and blood can love an insubstantial ghost."

"Then are you reconciled?" she asked.

He made a long and breathless pause, and fixed his gaze upon her with a depth of longing piteous to see.

"I am reconciled," he said at last.

"Love *sans* consummation is poor love," she said. "We cannot touch, far less embrace. But there is music, which of all the human Arts, creates a bridge that spans the gulf from mind to soul. Play," she bade, as she embraced her lute. "Play, and watch me as I vanish from you as a vapor into air. And so, farewell."

She struck a chord, that lingered for an instant, as it melded into other chords and other notes whose union bore into the world the short and dainty piece, *A Fantasia for Two Lutes*. In perfect sympathy he took his part, as Ghost and Man begat a child, compounded half of heaven, half of earth. Measure by measure, note by note, the ghostly part dissolved from view, and with it every aspect of the perfect light of which its bearer was the source.

And thus she vanished as they played. Fainter grew her face and form, by slow degrees, her light supplanted by a different light, familiar to the sense. Her features faded, reappeared, then faded once again, until the sounding of the final chord, at which the light of day shone fully in his eyes, and he beheld a different face, and heard his name repeated with a sound that fell upon his ears as sweetly as the voice that had bidden him farewell.

XXV.

"Aaron?" spoke the voice, neither urgent nor alarmed. "Aaron? Are you there?"

He started visibly, as one who wakens from a swoon, and looked bemusedly to see Melissa hovering above, and smiling pleasantly.

"I came to visit, Aaron, and to wish you Merry Christmas. But you were nowhere to be found, so I thought I'd peek in here. And so I've found you, but how strange you look! Are you quite well?"

He smiled and glanced about. Sunlight filled the sanctuary space, the brightest light of all the lights within the world of Form. His lute was cradled loosely in his arms and still he sat upon the chair where he had sat throughout his discourse with the shade of Margaret. Melissa now sat opposite, where Margaret had sat, smiling on him, but with furrowed brow, as if she half-suspected things were not quite right.

"What a strange experience I've had!" he cried, as up he rose and gently on the altar laid his lute, face down. "I've been in Heaven, and I've been in Hell. It's nothing like you think. Melissa, did you know that Hell was a cathedral — a Gothic cathedral? I . . . ." But here he stopped, perhaps because he saw the pretty eyes regarding him with deep concern, of a sort reserved for people who have lost their minds.

"Of course I dreamt it all," he said, in tones unlike the tones of someone who had lost his mind. "Yes . . . perhaps I did, but it was all so real! I was at your house last night . . . your mother gave me wine. Not just one glass, but two, and it was *very* strong, though good, quite good. Of course I wasn't used to it . . . it went right to my head. I'd never in my life drunk wine, but do you know what Melissa? I think I'll soon be drinking it again, and doing lots of things I never did before! It's Christmas, isn't it?"

"Yes, of course," Melissa said.

"You invited me to dinner," he observed.

"I did. As always. But you . . . ."

"And breakfast?" he cut in. "I'm genuinely starved! I haven't had a thing since yesterday!"

She seemed pleased to hear him say this, and she smiled like sunshine on a crisp Fall day.

"Breakfast is waiting," she replied. "What do you like? There's everything under the sun . . . sausage, bacon, eggs, pancakes, fried potatoes . . . we never stint on Christmas!"

"And so you shouldn't stint! You shouldn't stint on any day, much less on Christmas Day! Is there coffee too?"

"There is," she said. "I thought you didn't drink . . . ."

"Oh yes I do! Drink, and eat, and any other pleasure that a person can indulge in modestly, and morally, without converting it to vice. There's something else, as well, now that I think of it. I'd like to have a conversation with your Dad, whom I've been putting off for years. I think he'd be intrigued by what I have to say."

He smiled and gave a laugh, then looked at her and gaily chimed, "Now what think you of *that*?"

"I think it's wonderful!" she cried, and smiled and laughed in sympathy. "But Aaron, there's a change in you," she said, more soberly. "I've never seen you look so . . . ."

"Happy?" he rejoined. The word resounded in his sparkling eyes.

"Why, yes! That *is* the word! Forgive me, Aaron, if I say I thought I'd never use the word, as it applied to *you*! What's happened? Is it just for now, or is it, as I hope, a lasting thing?"

"I've seen a ghost, Melissa," he confessed. "Dream or not, it's all the same . . . that ghost has set me free. The fetters of my mind are stricken off and cast away. The offshoot? Happiness! Happiness for now, and then beyond, for never doubt there *is* a life beyond, and let no sophist tell you otherwise! I've seen the Devil too, and fought with him and won! What do you say? Is that explanatory?"

"Explanatory, yes," she said, amazed. "But not *quite* satisfactory."

"Ah, Melissa!" Aaron sighed. "Of course it's not. Let me take another tack. Have you ever read a book, and when you reached its ending knew exactly what the author had in mind, but couldn't put it into words? Such is Art, Melissa . . . thoughts and visions needing more than narrative in order to convey them from the artist's mind into the minds of others. My story is a work of art — unable to be grasped in just a word. Later at some quiet time I'll tell it to you in the form of art, but now, since I can see that you're ablaze with curiosity, I'll try the best I can to tell it in a word. Someone I know did something very bad — unthinkably, horribly bad — and somehow I believed myself to blame, although I didn't know what he had done, or that I'd had a part in it. And now this dream has come . . . a dream? No, I won't call it that. A dream is senseless and irrational, but this was not, fantastic though it was. A dream? I can't believe it; *won't* believe it! Never mind that now. In short, I'm changed. I'll never be the same, and good for me!"

"Then bravo!" cried Melissa, with her features all aglow. "Bravo, Aaron Westwode! Now let's go to breakfast, eh? I'll take you home, and won't they be surprised! Then after dinner you can sit with me and let me hear your story as a piece of art, and then I'll surely understand it all! As well as if I'd lived through it myself! And if you'd like, we . . . ."

Suddenly she drew up short. Her keen eyes narrowed, and she looked confused.

"Aaron . . . what is that?" She pointed to the nave. There upon a pew reposed an object, resting in plain sight—an object made of wood. Impulsively she looked toward the altar. Her eyes returned as quickly to the object in the nave.

"Is that a lute?" she breathlessly inquired.

At once she stepped into the nave, while Aaron kept his place above.

"That's just my case," he said, dismissively. "I left it there last night."

"It *is* a lute case," she affirmed. "But Aaron, there's a lute inside."

And so there was indeed. She took it from the case and turned it half-about, then looked it up and down, as if in admiration of its perfect form. Then back to Aaron she returned, where now he stood entranced.

"Is this your lute?" she asked.

For many moments he reflected, staring mutely at the lute, not striving to remove it from her hands. Finally he spoke.

"My lute is *there*," he said, and slightly moved his head toward the altar where it lay.

"But whose is this?" Melissa asked. "For this one is identical to yours!"

"I understand it all," he quietly declaimed, not speaking to Melissa, but uttering the words toward the empty nave. "Margaret, I never doubted you, nor ever will." His voice rose; his eyes addressed the rafters up above. His mien was that of trancelike ecstasy. "No signs and wonders will I ever need to keep your counsel in my heart and soul. Melissa, don't you see? No, how can you see, with only eyes? I'll tell you nonetheless. That lute is hers, created by the power that created mine, the power that created all the substance of the stars."

And still he gazed aloft, into the rafters and beyond. Nor did he turn and face the woman he addressed, but spoke to her as if she hovered somewhere in the space above, wherein his eyes were fixed.

"Her name is Margaret . . . *was* Margaret, because the part of her that bore that name is dead and gone. She died because my brother murdered her, and I was his accomplice . . . his accomplice, yes, although I never knew what I had done, or how I had been used by him. The Devil came to me, and whispered in my ear. He goaded me with hints and innuendoes, all to lead me to conclude that I was bad, corrupt; a blot upon the holy name of everything Divine. Yes! And I believed him, for he played upon the very sense of goodness that he sought to denigrate in me. My modest life and self-denial served to mask the guilt I felt within. I turned them into virtues of a sort, as if they were atonement for my sins that never were. Devoid of all hope, I yearned for death. I found my brother's note, in which he mocked my faith and vowed to end his life. Last night I stood upon the brink . . . the threshold of despair. And then she spoke to me, and I was saved."

Still to the rafters did he speak.

"I found her in this place, enrobed in light. She has no substance, only light, and such a light it is! Shall I describe it now? I can't! Melissa, what are words? She showed me things that eyes could never see, nor words relate, though words are all I have to tell you what I saw! She played her lute, the lute you now are holding in your hands, for music is a bridge that spans the gulf from mind to soul. Her music . . . *our* music . . . wafted me from time to time, and place to place and showed me things I never, ever thought could be. Melissa! What is that I hear? Is that the voice of a lute? Melissa, can you hear? I hear it now, as clean and pure and bright as ever it was played by ghostly hands, upon a ghostly instrument of wood!"

He stood enchanted, eyes still focused on the rafters overhead.

"I hear it!" he exclaimed, and smiled with childlike joy.

"So loud . . . so clear! *The Tremolo Fantasy* . . . a Dowland piece! She played it for me once before. Ach, listen to me! Once *before*? Last night, when all the world was fast asleep, and time stopped in its tracks! How like her now to come to me, with sweet sounds such as only she could make! Melissa, can you hear those notes that ring so clear to me? I fear you never can, and never will! Forgive me, please, and try to understand. She is my true salvation and my love, my only love. I will love her to the grave, and far beyond. Can I see her? No. Can I touch her? No. But love endures beyond mortality, beyond the sense, beyond the mortal compass of the mind. All things must change, yet she will be the same. And so we too must change, and still remain the same. Melissa, be my friend, my faithful friend, and I will be a friend to you. But understand, I have a single love, and that one love is barren of all shape, and dwells beyond the limits of the world!"

Suddenly, capriciously, he ceased to speak, and quickly turned about. He turned, he looked, and drew his breath in with a gasp.

Melissa sat within the holy space, where once the ghost of Margaret had sat, the lute enfolded in her arms. And from that lute sweet music issued forth — the music he had heard — created by Melissa's hands, with perfect grace and ease. *The Tremolo Fantasy* indeed she played, with verve and gusto in the act. In quiet awe he looked upon her as she carried on into its vibrant tremolo, with every note distinctly audible. Masterfully she played, and perfectly, with ease and comfort in her form and attitude. She finished with a six-part chord, that lingered in the air, then rose up from her seat, and looked directly into Aaron's eyes, with modesty depicted in her own.

For one full minute he regarded her as one whom he had never seen before. Motionless she held her place. Then, wordlessly, he went to her, and gently from her hands removed the lute. He turned it to and fro, and closely gave it scrutiny, as if he would discern by what strange agency the music it had played had come to be. He ran his hands along its length, and lightly plucked the open strings while listening with bated breath for something, so it seemed, in affirmation of a thought he had in mind. Finally he turned toward the altar, where with tender touch he laid the lute beside its perfect twin, and turned again to face the pretty one whose brilliant eyes retained their calm and peaceful shine.

Now straight into those eyes he peered, as if he were a sage, and she his crystal ball.

"Margaret?" he whispered, anxiously.

"Melissa," she replied.

"Margaret," he spoke aloud, as if it were a fact.

"Melissa," she replied.

He paused again in contemplation.

"But why?" he asked at last. "And how?"

"It . . . it's simple," she declared.

"How, simple?" he inquired.

"*Unfathomably simple*," she replied.

He gave a little start, then caught himself, and sought her eyes again. Though motionless, the eyes were eager, and they smiled. He shyly lifted both his hands, and touched her head, her hair, her shoulders and her cheeks. Then, as if content in the conclusion he had drawn, he chastely kissed her lips and pressed her to his heart.

Wordlessly, by one consent, they took each other by the hand, and walked together down the steps into the nave. And so they trod, still hand-in-hand, from aisle to vestibule and through the doors, into the Christmas air.

Morning sun shone brightly from atop the hills behind the river's edge. The air was dry, and cool, with not a vestige left of last night's snow. They walked along the graveyard path until they came to Aaron's small abode, at which they paused and kissed before proceeding on in the direction of Melissa's home.

* * *

BUT AS THEY drew away, a movement could be seen, within the entry of the little house. The door was opened from within, and from within the figure of a man emerged and stopped upon the threshold for a trice. The black man stood there, dressed in white, who in a moment stepped beyond the threshold to the path. He lingered there in somber reverie, as wistfully he watched the happy pair — not conscious of their being watched — while slowly they retreated out of view.

Then suddenly he clenched his fists, and gave a vicious snarl. Beneath his breath he swore a hateful oath, then raised one leg above his waist and brought it crashing hard upon the ground. He stomped so hard that presently a fissure opened up beneath his foot. With yet another snarl he closed his eyes and spun upon his heel. His substance turned into a twirling mist, which like a whirlpool drained into the crevice that his jealous rage had formed. In a twinkling he was gone. And never was he seen, in that dark form, upon the earth again.

THE END